FLASH THE SHEEP DOG

FLASH THE SHEEP DOG

by
KATHLEEN FIDLER

Illustrated by
ANTONY MAITLAND

CANONGATE · KELPIES

First published in Great Britain in 1965
by the Lutterworth Press.

First published in Kelpies, an imprint of
Canongate Books Ltd, in 1984
Sixth impression 1998

British Library Cataloguing-in-Publication Data
A catalogue record of this book is available upon request from
the British Library.

ISBN 0 86241 071 1

Printed and bound in Great Britain
by Caledonian International, Glasgow

CANONGATE BOOKS
14 HIGH STREET, EDINBURGH

Contents

I TOM GOES TO BIRKHOPE

"YOU'LL write to me, Tom?"

The small sandy-haired boy with freckles nodded.

"You've got the American address in your notebook all right?" his sister asked.

Tom Stokes nodded again. He wished the guard would wave his flag and let the train get on its way. Though he was miserable at parting with Kate, he hated this prolonged leave-taking.

"You know, Tom, I'd take you with me to America but there isn't time to make arrangements now—and—and I haven't got the money for your fare out there."

"I'll be all right, Kate. Don't worry!" For Kate's sake Tom managed to smile.

"Give my love to Uncle John and Aunt Jane. They'll be glad to see you," Kate sought to reassure him with assumed brightness.

Tom said nothing and the colour mounted in Kate's face. "You know I don't really want to leave you behind, Tom. It's just that Hymer—Hymer——"

"Hymer won't be expecting you to bring a kid brother along with you when you arrive in America to get married." Tom said with flat honesty.

Tears sprang to Kate's eyes. "I shall send for you, Tom, just as soon as Hymer says the word and I've saved up the fare."

"I'll be all right, Kate." He pressed his lips close together but a close observer might have seen that the corners of his mouth were trembling, despite the bravado of his twelve years.

"If only Aunt Susan hadn't died when she did, it would have given me time——" Kate began again.

"Please don't fuss, Kate." Tom felt if she said any more, he might begin to weep too. If he let Kate know how unhappy he was at parting with her, she might postpone her arrangements for going to America, and Tom knew what that meant to her.

"You'll like it up there at the farm," she said persuadingly.

"If I don't, I can always run away," Tom said with a laugh.

"Oh, Tom, you mustn't do that!" Kate sounded troubled.

"Cheer up, Kate! Maybe I was just kidding you."

The bustle of King's Cross station grew more intense; folk crowding round the tea-trollies on the platform snatched up their tea and cartons of orange juice and fled hurriedly to their compartments. Kate gave Tom a quick peck of a kiss and rushed out to the platform. Tom called to her through the window, "Don't worry about me, Kate. I'll get by. I hope you like America."

The guard was waving his green flag.

"Remember to write to me!" came the last imploring cry from Kate. She ran alongside the train as it began to move, waving to him. Tom waved back; the train gathered momentum and Kate stopped running and stood, a disconsolate dwindling figure on the platform.

Though to Kate Tom had tried to seem tough, he suddenly felt very alone and he stared hard through the window so that no one in the compartment should see how near he was to weeping. Soon the train left behind the soot-begrimed walls and the maze of streets. They passed a suburb of newly-built houses with gardens and a belt of green lawns. Tom watched the stations roar upon the train and sink back behind it. He thought of all that had happened in the last few weeks. It had all begun with the sudden death of Aunt Susan with whom Tom and Kate lived. Aunt Susan had brought them up after the death of their parents in a road accident.

All Kate's arrangements to sail to New York and marry Hymer Scanlon had been made before Aunt Susan died. If she put off her sailing now, it might be some time before she could get another passage; and she could not take Tom with her. They could not stay long in their present home either for the flat had been rented in Aunt Susan's name and the landlord gave them notice because he wanted to sell it. Kate was at her wits' end to know what to do with Tom. Then, all at once, she found a solution to her problem.

She came on a bundle of old letters while turning out

cupboards and drawers. They were from Aunt Susan's brother, a sheep farmer in the south of Scotland. There were not many letters and it was several years since the last one was written. On an impulse Kate sat down and wrote to John Meggetson and told him of his sister's death and her own predicament. To her surprise an answer came quite soon.

John Meggetson had turned the letter over to his wife, Jane. After she had read it she said, "The poor lassie does seem to be in a fix. I'm thinking we must do something to help her, John. Maybe we could have the laddie here till she's got settled in America? She says she'll send for him as soon as she's able."

"Aye," John agreed. He was a man of few words and usually left the talking to his wife.

"There's plenty of room for him here and I'd like to have a bairn about the house. I miss our own lassies now they're married."

"Will he not find it strange here after London?" John asked.

"Och, he'll soon get used to it! There's plenty on a farm to interest a lad. Write and tell Kate we'll not see her stuck and that we'll take the boy for a while. After all, he's your own sister's son and we ought to do something for him."

"Aye, that's so," John Meggetson agreed.

"Then just you put pen to paper and tell Kate to speak with us on the phone to make arrangements. She could put Tom on the train and you could fetch him from Edinburgh."

As the train sped north Tom began to wonder what the new home in Scotland would be like. Birkhope was the name of his uncle's farm. Birkhope? Tom's imagination began to turn Birkhope into a mansion surrounded by parklands. Kate had said that Uncle Meggetson was "not badly off". Tom's fancy magnified this into great wealth.

Perhaps his uncle went hunting on a great horse with hounds baying at his heels? Perhaps a fine river ran through the parklands of Birkhope? Maybe rich Uncle John would have a boat on the river too? Perhaps he would have a cabin cruiser like Tom had seen on the Thames at Richmond? Tom's mind went racing on from dream to dream of wealth and exciting living.

His uncle had told Kate he would meet Tom at Waverley Station with a car. What kind of a car? Tom finally decided on a Jaguar, a sleek Jaguar that would purr along the road to Birkhope. Here Tom's dreams became a little confused and the purr of the Jaguar mingled with the rumpetty-tum of the train and soon he was fast asleep in his corner.

After Newcastle the railway began to follow the coast and Tom got tantalizing glimpses of the sea. The train crossed the Tweed at Berwick and minutes later they were in Scotland. Tom looked through the window, feeling more strange and bewildered with every mile the train sped north. The country was so different from London, so empty, so lonely. Tom had no idea there were places like this, without houses and people. He felt a strange misgiving. What would Birkhope be like? When they reached the Firth of Forth he felt more reassured. At least here was a big estuary, wider even than the Thames, with ships coming and going on it. Where there were ships there must be docks and harbours too. There would still be a river to watch and streets to roam, and perhaps other boys to go wandering with him?

At last the train passed between streets of high crowding tenements and roaring through a canyon of high stone walls, drew into Waverley Station.

Tom lifted his battered suitcase from the rack and followed the rest of the passengers out of the train. He stood on the platform, a bewildered small boy, with the people surging past on either side of him like the eddies in a mountain stream. Tom looked about him desperately. However would he find his uncle among all these people? He followed the crowd to the platform exit and was almost the last to step through the barrier. Suddenly someone tapped him on the shoulder.

"Hullo, laddie! Are you Tom Stokes?"

Tom sprang round to face a stocky, sturdy man in a shabby tweed suit. His face was brown and weather-beaten, his eyes blue and keen as if used to looking into far distances.

Tom swallowed a little. "Y—yes, I'm Tom Stokes," he stammered.

"I thought you were. I recognized you from your photograph. I'm your Uncle John."

Tom shook hands rather limply with John Meggetson. His heart sank a little, for this was not a bit like the rich uncle of his dreams.

"This way, Tom. I'll take your case. I've got the farm wagon on the ramp going out of the station. It's a job to get parked anywhere near the station these days."

The "wagon" was a rather battered Land Rover which had seen good service on the farm.

"Hop in next to the driver's seat: here, beside me," Uncle John said.

There was a distinct smell of sheep inside the Land Rover. The seat at the back had been taken out and instead there was a square space from which a large ram glared balefully at Tom. Tom wrinkled his nose at the smell of sheep droppings.

"I heard there was a good ram for sale at the cattle market at Gorgie today so I took the opportunity to buy it while I was in Edinburgh," John Meggetson explained. "Do you know anything about sheep?"

Tom shook his head. After that the conversation dropped, for John Meggetson was busy extricating his wagon from the maze of traffic that rattled over the Waverley Bridge. He took a turn to the left up a steep street, then out into a road lined with big shops. Tom stared through the car window. Edinburgh looked a sizable place. It might be fun to explore it.

"Do you come to Edinburgh often, Uncle John?" he asked.

"No. Only now and again to the cattle market at Gorgie."

Tom was silent for a while, then he asked, "Is there a river at Birkhope?"

"Not exactly a river. There's a burn runs down to the Tweed."

"A *burn?*" Tom sounded puzzled.

"Maybe in England you call it a stream. Why, are you interested in fishing?" Mr. Meggetson's voice brightened.

"Do you fish from a boat?" Tom asked eagerly.

"No, no, laddie! I just put on my waders and step out a bit from the river bank. If you'd like to learn, maybe some evening I could show you how to cast a fly. Trout fishing, ye ken?"

Tom shook his head. He could hardly understand what Uncle John was saying, for his accent was so different from the way people talked in London. Conversation languished. On the road shops gave way to houses, then houses to fields and before long they were in the country. Soon wide moors lined each side of the road. To Tom the landscape seemed more and more lonely and desolate with each mile they covered. Green rounded hills, looking rain-washed, faded into the blue of the horizon. Uncle John nodded towards them.

"Great country, this, for sheep. Thousands of them bred on those hills!"

"Is there anything *besides* sheep?" Tom asked, his heart sinking slightly.

"Most farmers keep a few milk cows and maybe the odd pig," Uncle John replied practically, thinking in terms of farming.

"But what do people *do* here?" Tom wanted to know.

"Do? I reckon most folk do farming. Sheep pay weel these days both for wool and mutton."

Tom lapsed into silence. There seemed nothing but sheep and hills, hills and sheep. As John Meggetson was a man of few words, he fell silent too. The road ran alongside a swift small river. The wagon turned off the high road and along a narrower road that climbed between the rounded green hills. They reached a gate across a muddy lane. "Just open the gate for me, lad," Meggetson said.

Tom got down and swung open the gate and the Land Rover drove through. Tom was about to climb in again when his uncle said in surprise, "You've not shut the gate, Tom! We've got to shut gates here or we'd have valuable animals straying to the high road. That's the first thing you'll have to learn—always to shut the farm gates."

His uncle sounded so stern that Tom quailed a little.

"Another few hundred yards and you'll be there. Your aunt will have a good meal for you," John Meggetson told him in a gentler voice. After all, he could not expect too much from a laddie who'd been brought up in London.

The Land Rover rounded a green hillock and they came on Birkhope, its small-paned windows glinting in the late afternoon sun. It was a square Scottish house with windows on each side of a central porch and dormer windows in the roof. To Tom they looked like watching eyes. He was surprised to find the house made of *stone*. He had expected to see a brick house such as those in London. Behind the house stretched the farm outbuildings; the byre with its cows; the hay barn; the grain shed; the hen-houses and a row of pens for sheep. All was neat, tidy and orderly. A few hundred yards away on a slight rise behind the house was a small wood of fir trees which sheltered the steading from the keen blasts of winter.

"Weel, laddie, this is to be your hame for a while," Uncle John said as he brought the wagon to a standstill before the door.

" 'Hame'?" Tom was puzzled by the new word.

"Home, you call it, maybe, south of the Border," Uncle John told him drily.

The door flew open and Aunt Jane appeared with welcoming out-stretched hand. "Ah, there you are, Tom! Come in, laddie! Come ben!" she said warmly.

Tom, shaking her hand, looked round, wondering who "Ben" might be. For a moment he thought it might be the ram that his uncle was hauling out of the back of the Land Rover, but surely his aunt would never invite a sheep into the house? Aunt Jane, however, led Tom into a large kitchen were a bright fire burned in an open grate. A black and white collie dog rose from the hearth-rug and came to sniff at Tom's legs.

"Now, Jeff, under the table with you!" Aunt Jane pointed to the table and Jeff obediently disappeared underneath it. The table was set with a tempting array of home-made scones and sponge cake.

"I'll show you your room first, Tom," Aunt Jane said briskly. "Bring up your suit-case."

Tom followed her upstairs to a square landing with several doors leading off it. Aunt Jane opened one of them. "This is your room, Tom. If you want a wash, the bathroom's across the landing. Don't be too long before you come down to the kitchen. Your uncle will be ready for his meat. He doesn't like to be kept waiting." She disappeared down the stairs again.

Tom looked round his room. There was a single bed with a spotless white counterpane and a white painted chair. Beneath the window were a couple of shelves for books and a small painted chest of drawers. A curtained recess served for a wardrobe. Tom looked round him with pleasure. It was bigger and brighter than the small cramped box-room he had had in London. He crossed to the window and opened it. It looked towards a hill upon which sheep were pastured. Beyond it, stretching to the sky, were other green hills with more sheep. Not a house was in sight! Tom thought of the noisy London street with its roar of traffic and felt suddenly homesick for it.

"Nothing but sheep!" he said with a sigh.

He stood staring at the cloud shadows chasing each other across the hill till he suddenly remembered his aunt's warning not to be too long. He rushed to the bathroom, had a quick wash, dashed a comb through his hair, then hurried downstairs.

Uncle John was already seated in his chair at the head of the table. With a hint of impatience in his voice he said, "Take your seat, lad!" and pointed to a chair at his right hand.

Aunt Jane lifted a big tureen of soup from the hob at the side of the fire and set it down at her place. She ladled plentiful helpings of broth from it and set the soup-plates before each of them, then took her own seat.

"Are we ready now?" Uncle John asked.

Tom took this as a signal to begin and lifted his soup-spoon, only to find Uncle John's eye upon him in a reproving stare of surprise.

"We'll ask a blessing first," his uncle said.

Tom put down his soupspoon as if it were red hot and it fell with a clatter to the floor. His uncle waited silently while Tom picked it up again. Tom, covered with confusion, blushed to the roots of his hair. In a slightly louder voice than usual Uncle John spoke rather a long grace. Once it was said, he gave himself to the serious business of eating.

"Come along, Tom! Take your broth. You'll be hungry after your long journey," Aunt Jane said kindly.

Tom tasted the broth. It was thick and full of vegetables, onions, carrot, turnips, shredded kale. It was quite unlike any soup he had had before. Kate's usual way of making soup was to slit open a packet. There was something rich and good about this soup his aunt had made, but Tom wished she had not given him quite such a big helping of it. His uncle had finished long before Tom had reached the bottom of his plate. Tom was worried about keeping them waiting but he did not like to leave any broth for fear of a reproof.

"Another helping, Tom?" his aunt asked.

"No, thank you," Tom replied quickly, but he hastened to add, "It's very good soup though. I've never had that kind of soup before."

'Aye, you uncle likes his sheep's heid broth," Aunt Jane remarked.

"Sheep's heid?" Tom repeated, wondering what on earth it was.

"Made from the head of a sheep," Aunt Jane explained. Immediately Tom felt a bit sick! How could anyone use such a horrible thing as a sheep's head to make soup? He wished he had not eaten all of it. Aunt Jane never noticed Tom's discomfiture, however, but removed the plates and set the second course before them. This time the plates were heaped with potatoes, mashed turnips and a strange kind of dark meat, something like a sausage without its skin.

"Ah! Haggis and bashed neeps!" Uncle John said with satisfaction. "D'ye like haggis, Tom?"

"I've never had it before," Tom said.

"Ah, then it'll be a new experience for ye," Uncle John said with a twinkle in his eye. "Did your Aunt Susan never make haggis?"

Tom shook his head.

"Maybe she couldna' get the right ingredients in London," Aunt Jane remarked.

"What are bashed neeps?" Tom asked cautiously.

His aunt laughed. "Och, laddie, it's just our name for mashed turnips."

Tom felt that at least he would be safe with the "bashed neeps" and potatoes. He ventured on a mouthful of the haggis.

"Like it?" Uncle John asked.

"I think so," Tom replied doubtfully, "but I'm not used to Scotch food."

"Now, now, Tom! You never use the word 'Scotch' except for whisky and oatmeal and seed potatoes," his uncle reproved him. "We use the words Scots and Scottish. We don't like to be called Scotch."

Tom was silent. It seemed that not only had he to get used to new food, but he had to learn a new language too. His uncle began to talk with his aunt about the prices sheep had fetched at the cattle market at Gorgie that day.

"Cheviot hoggs were doing better the day. They reached a price of eight pounds, seventeen shillings."

"No' bad!" Aunt Jane remarked with interest. "You should do well with the young flock when you come to market them."

Tom toyed with his haggis. He was not really sure that he liked it. He felt something sniffing at his legs and peeped under the table. It was the collie dog, Jeff. Tom put down a hand and the dog licked it. Tom felt grateful for this friendly sign. Watching his chance, he quickly put down a portion of haggis to the dog. It was gobbled up quickly. There was another lick at Tom's hand and again he secretly gave the dog another mouthful. He was not so fortunate with the third. The dog wagged his tail and Uncle John felt the movement under the table. He caught Tom red-handed giving Jeff another portion from his plate.

"Tom! What are you doing feeding the dog?" he demanded sternly.

"I—I just gave him a bit," Tom stammered.

"Now, look here, lad! If there's one rule I make, it is that my dog shall never be fed from my table. Scrap feeding like that could be the ruin of a good sheep dog. I'll not have it, mind! My dogs get one good meal a day when they've finished their work and that's that! I know you're new to our ways, Tom, but it's better to have this straight from the start. Ye're not to feed my dogs without my permission, understand."

Tom pushed his plate back. He felt he had no more appetite for any food.

"D'you not like the haggis, Tom?" his aunt asked. There was a kindly understanding in her voice.

"I—I'm not sure," Tom said.

"A bit sponge, then?" She pointed to the sponge cake. "There's real cream in it," she said temptingly.

Tom gave in. "Yes, please."

The cream cake was good. At least he was all right with Aunt Jane's baking, but once he had finished that, Tom could eat no more. He fidgeted in his chair as he waited for his uncle to finish eating. He seemed to make an enormous meal. Tom wondered if, like his dogs, he only took one

meal a day! At last his uncle sat back satisfied and took out his pipe.

"Go take a look round the farm if you've a mind, Tom," he said.

Tom went outside, followed by Jeff. He strolled round the hen-houses and wandered into the empty byre. The cows were in the field by the stream. He inspected the barn and grain shed. The farm machinery in the big shed attracted his attention.

"I wonder what this thing's for?" he said aloud when he came on a mechanical seed-planter. Living in a city all his life, the things that were commonplace objects to a country child were mysteries to him. He went out of the farm-yard, then rushed back again.

"Gosh! I almost forgot to shut that gate! I don't want to get into Uncle John's black books any more."

He wandered down to the "burn"—the small swiftly-flowing stream. In a pool a fish plopped, marking the evening rise, but to Tom that meant nothing. He stood by the stream dreaming of the wide London River, alive with ships and barges, tug boats and swift launches. A great wave of longing for London engulfed him. When he remembered the noisy streets of Poplar and the friends who played among them with him the utter quiet of the hills seemed to stifle him. He thought of Kate, too, and how they used to wander round the London markets together and his heart felt like a heavy weight. There seemed nothing but emptiness in the wide greenness of the hills. Suddenly a cold nose was thrust into his hand. It belonged to Jeff. Tom knelt down beside the dog and patted him and Jeff licked his hands and face.

"If only Uncle John had let me feed you!" Tom whispered.

Up at the farm his uncle was speaking about him to his
aunt.

"He's a strange laddie. I wonder how he'll settle here."

"Och, give him time," Jane Meggetson said indulgently.
"He's a town-bred laddie and it's all new to him. Once he's
got used to our country ways, he'll come out of his shell.
Remember he's been torn up by the roots."

"Aye, maybe you're right, lass."

"He's taken a right liking to Jeff, though," Jane said,
peering through the window. "He's down by the meadow
now, fair making a fuss of the dog."

"I hope he doesna' make a *fool* of the dog," John Meggetson growled. "I don't want the dog spoiled with over
much petting."

"Aye, but you were a bit hard on the lad at supper-time,
John, when he gave Jeff a bit of his haggis. He's got all to learn
yet. I think you shouldna' have spoken to him so sharply."

"Better to have things straight from the first!"

"Aye, but go easily. He's coming in now."

Tom came in, followed by Jeff. John Meggetson pointed
his finger and the dog sat down obediently at his feet. There
was perfect understanding between him and his master.

"You seem to have made friends with Jeff," Aunt Jane
smiled at Tom.

"He's a nice dog," Tom said guardedly.

Tom took out the comic he had been reading in the train
and sat down and read it all through again. After that there
seemed to be nothing to do. He fidgeted a bit then said,
"If—if you don't mind, I think I'll go to bed."

"Why, it's early yet," Aunt Jane was beginning, then
stopped and added, "I expect you're tired after that long
journey."

"I was going to suggest that you went up the hill with

me to bring down a few sheep for tomorrow's sale at Peebles," his uncle said, "but if you're tired, just away to your bed, lad."

Tom hesitated for a minute, then took this as an order and said "Good night, Aunt Jane. Good night, Uncle John," in a very correct manner and went up the stairs.

John Meggetson got up from his chair. "I'll away up the hill and fetch the sheep," he said in a slightly disappointed voice.

Tom leaned his elbows on the sill of his bedroom window and watched his uncle and Jeff go up the hill. He wished now that he had asked to go with them. As they approached the small flock his uncle halted. He made a sweeping gesture with his arm away to the right and like lightning Jeff was running in a wide semi-circle to get behind the sheep. At a whistle from John Meggetson he stopped, crouched low on his stomach and began to crawl in nearer towards the sheep. The animals began to move down the hill. Without hurrying or harrying them, Jeff followed behind, heading off stragglers. Back and forth he ran behind the sheep till they reached John Meggetson. He shouted an instruction to Jeff who herded the sheep neatly through the farmyard gate and turned them into a sheep pen. Not till the last straggler was safely gathered in, did Jeff relax his efforts. Meggetson patted the dog. "Weel done, Jeff! Weel done, lad!" Jeff gave a quick lick at his hand. To him his master's word of praise meant everything.

Tom leaned out of his window and watched, his interest held at last. His eyes never left the dog till he disappeared round a corner of the house.

"If only I'd a dog like that——" Tom sighed. "It might not be so lonely here then." He thought of Kate and pressed his lips firmly together for a moment. "Don't worry, Kate!" he said in a whisper to himself. "I'll do my best."

2

THE FRIDAY MARKET
AND WHAT CAME OF IT

THE NEXT FEW days Tom mooned about the farm. He tramped to the top of the nearest hill but from it he could only see a succession of similar green hills, dotted everywhere with sheep. Tom felt he would soon grow to hate sheep! He went down to the stream and tried guddling for trout but without success. He dreamed all the time of the wide river he had left behind and the great noisy city. He was homesick for the sights and sounds of the London streets and the friends he had left behind.

"What is there to *do* here?" he asked himself miserably.

His aunt watched him with concern. She gave him jobs to do, feeding the hens and collecting eggs; weeding the kail-yard and the tiny garden where she grew flowers. She thought if she kept him occupied she would keep him happy. Tom did her bidding willingly, but without interest.

"The lad's just plain bored here, John," she told her husband.

"Maybe he'll brighten up when the school reopens after the holidays."

"Yes, perhaps he'll make friends at school," Mrs. Meggetson agreed. "It's a pity it's the holidays and a long time till the school reopens again."

"He seems to brighten up when he takes Jeff for a walk," Meggetson remarked.

"Aye, he's right fond of the dog. Are you going to the Friday market tomorrow, John?"

"Yes, I've a parcel of lambs to take to the sales."

"Could you take Tom into Peebles with you? It would make a bit of a change for him. It might interest him."

"Och! You worry over much whether the lad is interested or not."

"I want him to settle down with us, John. There's something likeable about the laddie."

"All right! I'll take him," John agreed.

The weekly stock market was held in Peebles, a small Border town nestling beside the River Tweed. The market was not a big one but the farmers attended it from the surrounding districts.

Tom and his uncle set off next morning with ten young sheep in the back of the farm wagon. Jeff lay beside Tom's feet at the front of the wagon. For part of the way the road followed the stream, dropping downhill towards the valley of the Tweed. When they came to the outskirts of the town, Tom began to look about him with more interest. Before long they reached the wide main street of Peebles, lined with shops on either side. The pavements were busy with shoppers and tourists, for Peebles had always been a favourite holiday place for the people of Glasgow and Edinburgh. Uncle John did not pull up in the High Street. The wagon turned to cross a wide bridge. Under the bridge a river swirled and eddied between steep banks.

"Nothing like the Thames, but it really is a river!" Tom said to himself.

At the other side of the bridge they turned right and before long they reached a lane. At the end of it was the Stock Market.

Tom's face dropped with disappointment. He had

imagined something like the Smithfield or Covent Garden markets. Here was a collection of haphazard buildings; a circular hall where the auction was held and a number of iron-fenced cattle pens. The pens were occupied by small droves of sheep and a few pigs and cattle.

Mr. Meggetson got down from the driving seat and Jeff followed at his heels as though well acquainted with the routine. He let down the back of the truck and bundled the sheep out. Jeff, bobbing behind, saw the sheep safely penned. John Meggetson had a word with the man in charge of the pens, then turned to Tom.

"Come along, Tom. We'll go to the ring and see what's going on there. It'll be quite a while before it's the turn of our sheep to be sold."

He led the way to the auction ring. As he opened the door, a babble of chatter met them from the already assembled farmers. Two or three tiers of seats sloped upwards like those at a circus. No one seemed to be sitting in the seats, though. Most of the farmers were clustered along the rail that bounded the ring.

"You climb up near the top tier and you can watch what's going on," Uncle John told Tom. "Mind, though, that you don't nod your head when the auctioneer starts or you might find you've bought a couple of pigs!" He laughed heartily at his own joke, but Tom felt he dare not move.

Above the ring was a kind of fenced pulpit. A tall man who had been talking with the farmers entered the "pulpit" and his clerk rang a brass hand-bell loudly. This was the signal that the auction was about to begin. Other farmers came hurrying into the seating enclosure. A stockman with a stout ash-plant stick took up a position in the centre of the sawdust-covered ring and three squealing pigs were driven in. Immediately the auctioneer started what seemed an incomprehensible gabble to Tom.

'Eight and six, eight and six, well, seven shillings I am bid. Seven and six, seven and six, eight shillings, eight and six——" His voice ran on at a monotonous level like an incantation.

After the pigs some young bullocks were auctioned, then came the turn of the sheep. There were several small droves, for five-month lambs were usually sold in August. Tom watched for a while and then he began to fidget. It seemed to be a long time before his uncle's animals came up for sale. His uncle would be there a while yet. Tom touched him on the arm. "Uncle John, I'd like to have a look at Peebles," he told him.

"Getting tired of the sale, lad? I'll need to stay by for a while yet till my sheep come up. You can go and have a look at the town, though. Meet me at one o'clock by the statue of the lion outside the Tontine Hotel in the main street. You canna' miss it. See you're there on time!"

Tom wriggled his way through the crowd at the door and hurried down the lane towards Peebles. At the bridge he paused to lean over and look down into the river. At one side it wound through a well-kept park; on the other house gardens came almost to its banks. Tom trudged on into the town and wandered about, looking at the shop windows. He found he felt almost as lonely in the town as at Birkhope. If only he had had a friend to join in his exploring! He stood by the kerbside watching the passing cars and all at once he felt homesick for the rush and swirl of London's traffic; for Poplar and the Thames that ran near the end of his street; for the lads who chased round the docks with him; for the great ships that sailed up Limehouse Reach to London Docks. The longing for London swept over Tom like a great wave. Suddenly a bus swung to a standstill by the kerb. It was labelled Edinburgh.

The conductor leaned out. "Getting on, laddie?" he shouted.

Tom discovered he was standing right at a bus stop. Edinburgh? From Edinburgh he could get to London! He still had the ten shillings in his pocket that Kate had given him as a parting gift. There had been nothing on which to spend it at Birkhope. On a sudden impulse he swung himself on to the bus! Maybe in Edinburgh he could stow away on a train to London? Once he was in London, perhaps he could find a job there if he pretended to be older than he was? The bus rolled way with Tom aboard.

A minute or two later John Meggetson's truck rumbled to a halt near the bus stop. The farmer got out and looked up and down the street. There was no small boy standing anywhere near the Tontine Hotel. No sign of Tom at all!

"Where can the lad be?" John Meggetson said to himself, searching the street with his eyes. "I told him to be here promptly. Surely he couldn't get lost in a small town like Peebles?"

Another farmer tapped him on the arm. "Looking for someone, John?"

"Aye, my nephew! The young rascal should have been here to meet me."

"Is that the sandy-haired laddie who was with you at the market?"

"Aye, that's the one!"

"I think I saw him get on the Edinburgh bus two or three minutes ago."

"The Edinburgh bus! Why, in the name of fortune, would the lad get on that? Are you certain, Bob?"

"Aye, pretty sure! He was the only lad at the market."

"Michty me! I'll have to go after him. I'll maybe over-take the bus. It'll have to stop now and again to pick folk up." John Meggetson was already up in the driver's seat and starting up the truck.

He had driven about three miles when he saw the bus ahead. It was stopping to take up passengers in the little village of Eddlestone. Meggetson drew up just ahead of the bus, jumped down from his truck and ran back to the stationary bus. He signalled to the driver to wait a minute, then mounted the bus.

Tom was sitting near the middle of the bus. He had not seen his uncle's truck pull ahead. Grim faced, John Meggetson marched up to him and took him by the shoulder.

"Where d'you think you're going, Tom?"

Tom turned quite pale. "I—I—Edinburgh——" he stammered.

John Meggetson looked grimmer than ever. "Up with ye!" he ordered. "Off the bus at once!" He took Tom by the elbow and jerked him to his feet. People stared at them. Tom had no choice but to leave the bus, as his uncle hustled him towards the door. The conductor rang the bell and the bus drew away.

"Weel, this is a nice carry-on!" Uncle John said, pushing Tom towards the truck. "I trust you to look round Peebles and you get on a bus for Edinburgh. What was the big idea?"

Tom felt suddenly ashamed. "I—I was wanting to go back to London," he faltered.

"Up on the truck with you! We'll talk about this when we reach Birkhope," his uncle said angrily.

Jeff was lying on the floor of the driving cab. He looked up when Tom climbed in and sniffed at him and thumped his tail in welcome. Tom put down a hand and rubbed Jeff gently behind the ears. John Meggetson gave the boy and the dog a curious sideways glance. He put the truck in reverse, then turned and drove back the way he had come.

They rattled through Peebles and took the road towards the hills. Uncle John did not speak and when Tom stole a glance at him, his face looked dark and forbidding. Tom turned his head away and stared at the road on his side of the truck. He felt thoroughly miserable.

Just ahead a small flock of sheep was huddled into a grassy lay-by off the road. Between them and the road, lying on the edge of the macadam, panting and squirming, was a small sheep dog. Something peculiar about the dog's attitude attracted Tom's attention.

"Stop, Uncle John!" he cried. "Please stop! I think there's something wrong with that dog minding those sheep!"

John Meggetson leaned forward to look, then he drew up the truck with a screech of brakes. He leaped down and ran to the dog. Tom jumped down after him. The dog gave a pitiful yelp. She struggled to rise, then flopped back on the road again.

"She's Bess! Matt Broughton's little bitch! What's up with her?"

John Meggetson examined her with gentle experienced hands. Her hind leg stuck out at an unusual angle.

"The wee animal's leg is broken!" Meggetson cried angrily. "She'll have been struck by a passing car as she herded the sheep out of the way of the traffic."

"Was she taking the flock along the road by herself?" Tom asked in surprise.

"That fool, Matt Broughton, will have stopped for a drink in the last pub we passed. He'll have left Bess to look after the flock. He's done it many a time, and I've warned him he'd do it once too often. He just laughs and says Bess can manage the flock as weel as he can. Now what's to be done? I'll have to get the poor wee animal to the vet in Peebles as soon as may be. I'll go rouse Matt Broughton out of the pub!"

He lifted the little collie with extreme tenderness and cradled her in his arms. She gave a little bark and looked towards the sheep still huddled in the lay-by.

"A clever wee lass she is! She's trying to tell me to look after her sheep. There was never a sheep dog with a greater sense of duty than Bess. A pity Broughton has no' the wits to look after her better!" John Meggetson considered for a moment, looking hard at Tom.

"Look, lad, if I leave you here with Jeff, d'you think you can look after these sheep till I get back?"

"I'll try," Tom said.

"Right! I'm trusting you, Tom."

He did not see the sudden grateful look that Tom threw at him for he was busy releasing Jeff from the driving cab. The old sheep dog looked from his master to the sheep and back again.

"Aye, Jeff! You're to watch the sheep. Do as Tom bids you." He clapped Tom on the shoulder to indicate that he was master.

A couple of cars whizzed by at high speed. "You'd be better off this main road," Meggetson said. "See, Tom, where the road forks?" He pointed in the direction. "The left fork leads to a side-road that goes to Broughton's farm. Could you drive the sheep along there? Jeff'll nearly do it for you."

"What would I have to do?" Tom asked doubtfully.

"Get my stick out of the truck and watch for the sheep straggling on either side. Just point with the stick and say 'Up Jeff!' and he'll pull in the stragglers. He'll maybe not even need a word. Leave Jeff to it."

"All right! I'll do my best," Tom said.

"Take your time and don't hurry the sheep."

John Meggetson swung himself into the cab of his truck and set Bess tenderly on the seat beside him. He watched Tom start out to drive the flock with Jeff weaving back and forth behind them. As soon as they were fifty yards on their way he started up the engine and reversed and turned back on the road to Peebles. He drew up at the inn he knew Matt Broughton frequented. He found him at the bar, glass in hand.

"A word wi' ye, Broughton!" John said abruptly. "Did ye leave some sheep by the roadside?"

"Aye, Meggetson, I did. What of it?" Broughton sounded aggressive.

"I've got your collie bitch in the cab of my truck. She's been injured."

"What's wrong?" Broughton asked sharply.

"We found her lying with her leg broken. She'd been hit by a passing car, no doubt. If I hadn't found you at the first cast I was on my way with her to the vet."

This was sobering news for Matt Broughton. Careless though he might be, he thought a lot of the little collie.

"Will you run us both in your truck to the vet, Birk-hope?"

It was often the custom among farmers to call each other by the names of their farms.

"Aye," Meggetson said briefly and led the way.

Matt Broughton lifted the little animal from the seat with infinite tenderness. She gave a quick yelp of pain in spite of his care but she licked his hand.

"Bess! Bess! I shouldna' have left you by yourself on the road," Broughton said contritely.

"You're right there, man!" Meggetson rebuked him.

"Whiles I think you don't deserve a good wee bitch like she is. She was still struggling to herd your sheep when we found her, squirming along on her stomach."

"D'you think the vet will be able to save her leg? He'll not have to destroy her, will he?" Matt asked anxiously.

"We'll soon see!" Meggetson replied grimly.

"I've been a fool!" Broughton blamed himself.

After an examination the veterinary surgeon stated that Bess's leg was broken in two places, but he could set the bone.

"She'll never run as she used to do at the sheep dog trials, though," he added.

"So long as she doesn't suffer and she's not lame! That's all I care about," Matt said contritely.

"You'd better leave her with me for a few days," the vet decided. "She'll rest better here than she would round the farm."

The two men left the surgery. "I'll run you along to your sheep, Broughton," John Meggetson offered.

"Thank ye, Birkhope."

Neither man spoke till they reached the road leading to Broughton's farm and sighted Tom plodding along behind the flock with Jeff.

"Who's the laddie, Birkhope?" Matt asked.

"My nephew. *He* spotted Bess lying injured by the roadside."

"A good thing he did! He's managing the sheep pretty weel."

"He's got sense enough to leave it to Jeff. He's got a liking for the dog."

"Weel, I'm grateful to the lad," Broughton commented.

With Jeff's help Tom had drawn the flock on to the grassy verge at the side of the road and stood waiting for them.

"Right, Tom!" his uncle said. "Mr. Broughton will take over now."

"Was Bess badly hurt?" Tom asked.

"A badly broken leg, but the vet says she'll recover," Broughton answered. "Thank ye for what ye did, lad."

"We'll be on our way now," Meggetson said. He whistled for Jeff. "I'll turn the wagon here."

"Thanks, Birkhope! I'll not forget what you've done for me this day," the rough farmer said, raising his hand in farewell.

When they reached the main road John Meggetson gave a quick look at Tom. "You did no' badly with Broughton's sheep, lad."

Tom made no reply but his eyes brightened. His uncle went on, "We'll say no more about this afternoon's trip, if you'll not do it again, Tom."

"I'll do my best, Uncle John," Tom promised. His heart felt lighter than it had done since he came to Scotland.

When they reached Birkhope Aunt Jane came out to open the farm-yard gate. "A long time you've been gone!" she remarked.

"Aye, we met with a bit of trouble." John told her about the injury to Broughton's collie.

"That Matt Broughton's a fool for the drink!" she exclaimed.

"I reckoned he'll stay sober next market day for he'll have no Bess to look after the flock for him. Give him his due, he's fond of her and he was right shaken to find what had happened. He's not a bad chap at heart."

"Och, you! You'd make excuses for your grandmother's murderer!" Jane teased him, but she looked at her husband with warm affection. "Your tea's ready, but I've no doubt you got a good dinner in Peebles," she remarked.

"Jings! We clean forgot our dinner!" Meggetson exclaimed.

Jane stared at him. "Guid sakes! What made *you* forget your dinner?"

Tom blushed guiltily as he thought of his bus ride, but Uncle John never turned a hair. "Och! It was just a matter of a young *sheep* that went astray," he said.

Aunt Jane was busy pouring out the tea and Uncle John caught Tom's eye. Slowly Uncle John closed one of his own eyes. Tom blinked in surprise. Surely Uncle John, quiet staid Uncle John, had never *winked* at him?

When Uncle John had smoked his pipe after the meal, he got up and said as usual, "I'll away up the hill to take a look at the sheep." Then, to Tom's surprise, he added, "Like to go up with me, Tom?"

Even more to his own surprise Tom answered, "Yes, Uncle John."

From the window Jane watched them go up the hill. "I wouldna' have believed it!" she said to herself. "That trip to Peebles must have done them both good."

A few days later a battered-looking car arrived at the farm gate. Aunt Jane looked out of the window. "Mercy me! If it isna' Matt Broughton!" she exclaimed.

Matt brought a puppy on a lead behind him to the door. "Good day to you all," he said. "Birkhope, I've come to thank you for what you did for Bess."

"Jings, man! There was no need to make a special journey, though you're welcome here," Meggetson told him. "How's Bess doing?"

"Fine! Just fine! She'll be able to follow the sheep again. You saved a valuable animal for me, Meggetson, and to show you I'm grateful I've brought you one of Bess's last litter. He's a good dog."

John Meggetson eyed the puppy as an expert in sheep dogs. "Aye, that's a good wee dog right enough. How old is he?"

"Coming on for six months. He comes of the best strain of Border Collies," Broughton said, not without pride. "If he's like Bess he'll not shame you when he comes to drive sheep. I'd like you to have him, Meggetson." He held out his hand and John shook it in friendly fashion.

"Thank you, Broughton. All the same, it was Tom here who saw the state Bess was in. I was driving the truck and might never have seen her. It was Tom who took along your sheep for you too. I think you should give the dog to him."

Tom gave a deep indrawn breath. Broughton turned to him. "Would *you* like to have the dog, lad?"

Tom could hardly trust his voice. "Oh, I would! I would!" he cried.

"Here, then, take him, he's yours!" Broughton put the lead into Tom's hand.

Tom knelt beside the silky-haired black and white puppy and put his arms round him. "Oh, thank you, Mr. Broughton!" He almost choked with gratitude. "What's his name?"

"I never gave him one. You can name him for yourself."

The little dog shot out a red tongue and licked Tom's cheek.

"See that! Out with his tongue like a flash!" Aunt Jane remarked.

"That's what I'm going to call him! *Flash!*" Tom exclaimed. "That shall be his name, Flash!"

"A good name for a sheep dog!" Uncle John nodded his approval. "A short name like that is best when you call after him on the hills. There's no sense in some of these fancy names that people give their show dogs. Imagine calling 'Come awa' to me, Wentworth of Montmorency!' The sheep would be over the next hill by the time you got it out."

For the first time since he came to Birkhope Tom found himself joining in a hearty laugh with his uncle.

That night, after supper, as Tom knelt on the hearthrug playing with Flash, John Meggetson asked, "What kind of a dog do you want Flash to be, Tom?"

"What do you mean, Uncle John? He's a sheep dog, isn't he?"

"Not a *proper* sheep dog till he's been trained for it. I mean, do you want him to be like Jeff, a working dog, or just a plaything for yourself."

Tom turned the matter over in his mind, then he asked his uncle plainly, "But he'd be more *your* dog than mine, wouldn't he, if *you* trained him to look after the sheep?"

John Meggetson appreciated the honesty of this reply. "Aye, he would, if *I* trained him, but if *you* train him, Tom, then he'll be yours for life. Understand, lad, I'm not wanting to take your dog from you."

"But I wouldn't know how to go about training him." Tom sounded worried.

"If you'll promise to abide by my instructions, then I'll show you, but you must do the bidding and handling of the dog."

Tom's face brightened. "I'll have a bash at it, Uncle John."

"That's a bargain, then. D'you know this, Tom? I wouldn't be bothering about the dog if I didn't know he comes of the best sheep-dog strain in the Scottish Borders. His mother, Bess, has taken many a prize in the Sheep Dog Trials. There's no reason why Flash shouldn't become a champion."

"Champion of what?" Tom looked quite bewildered.

"Do you mean to tell me you've never heard of Sheep Dog Trials?"

Tom shook his head. Uncle John looked amazed.

"Guid sakes! What do they teach you in London? Sheep Dog Trials? They're held all over Britain wherever you get sheep farms. There's an International Sheep Dog Society arranges these trials and folk enter their dogs to take part in a Trial Meeting."

Light began to dawn on Tom. "You mean the dogs enter for a competition, something like a Sports Meeting?"

"That's the way of it, only the Trials are concerned with the kind of thing the dogs do in their everyday work, fetching sheep in, driving them and herding them into a pen."

Tom looked interested. "And the dog that does the best becomes the champion?"

"Aye, but he's got to run in his local Trials first and win there before he can enter the big International Trials."

"A bit like winning a heat to get into the final race?"

"That's the idea. Only the dogs winning qualifying Trials can enter for the Supreme Championship. Folk who enter their dogs for the Trials have to be members of the Sheep Dog Society and have their dogs registered in the Society's books."

"Does it cost much to be a member?" Tom asked.

"A pound to join and a pound subscription each year."

Tom's face fell. "Then I can't enter Flash. I haven't got two pounds."

Uncle John was silent for a minute or two. "Maybe we could find a way round that," he said at last. "You could give your aunt a bit of help with the hens, and whiles do a bit of weeding in the kail-yard, and I'd be willing to advance the two pounds as wages."

Tom's face lit up. "Why, yes, I'll do that. Thank you very much, Uncle John."

"You'll stick by your bargain?" Uncle John gave him a searching look.

"I promise!" Tom answered firmly.

"Right! I'll send in your name to the Sheep Dog Society as the owner of Flash."

Tom's eager freckled face beamed. "When can we start training Flash?"

"Tomorrow! There's one thing you'll no' have to do, though."

"What's that?"

"I saw you slipping the dog a wee bit of your aunt's chocolate cake at tea-time. Now, your aunt's chocolate cake is too good for the dog, or else the dog's too good for your aunt's chocolate cake, whichever way you like. You'll have to stop that, Tom, or you'll spoil the dog."

Tom looked slightly ashamed. Nothing escaped Uncle John!

"Flash'll be like a man training for a race, mind! A fat dog'll not win anything, any more than a fat man. One meal a day, only, like Jeff has. Mind, now!"

"All right, Uncle John, I'll mind that," Tom promised, not realizing that for the first time he was using a Scottish turn of speech like Uncle John's.

3 FLASH'S TRAINING BEGINS

"MAYBE WE COULD make a start on training your dog. I've got half an hour I can spare afore I look to the sheep," John Meggetson said after breakfast next day. "The first thing he has to learn is to answer to his name and to walk behind ye."

Tom got up from the hearthrug where he had been kneeling beside the black and white puppy, rubbing him gently behind the ears. "I think he knows his name already, Uncle John. Watch this!" Tom lifted his voice a little. "Hi, Flash!"

The dog lifted his head alertly.

"Very good!" Uncle John nodded his approval. "He'll be quick to learn, that one. Now he'll have to go on his lead." He took the lead down from a hook on the wall and snapped it on to the dog's collar and handed the end of it to Tom. "We'll take the dog outside to the paddock."

"Come on, Flash!" Tom said, giving a little jerk to the lead. Flash rose to his feet. The minute Uncle John opened the door, however, Flash made a rush for it, tugging Tom along with him.

"No, no, Flash! That'll not do! It's for your master to lead you, no' for you to lead your master."

Flash continued his headlong rush outside. John Meggetson followed. "Hold on to him, Tom. I'll just get my stick."

Tom looked shocked. "You—you'll not beat him, Uncle John? He's *my* dog. You wouldn't dare! I'll—I'll——" Tom almost choked.

"Steady on, lad! Ye rush at a thing faster than your wee dog! Of course I shall not beat him! The stick's to guide him, no' to thrash him. I've never found cause to thrash one of my dogs yet."

Tom felt rather foolish. "Sorry, Uncle John!"

"Aye, weel, I'm more pleased than vexed at your outburst, laddie." Uncle John became serious. "But you've never to let me catch *you* thrashing your dog, either. No good sheep dog was ever made out o' a cowed animal yet. You've to be *firm* wi' him, but never let anger get the better of you. Now, take the stick in your hand and do as I bid ye."

Tom took the stick. Flash looked at it out of his eye corner but showed no fear.

"Now pull the dog *behind* you on the lead and at the same time say plainly, 'Come behind, Flash!' Hold the lead tight."

Flash, however, had made up his mind that Tom meant to go for a walk and he bounded ahead.

"Come behind, Flash!" Tom called loudly, pulling hard on the lead. Flash was brought up short but he strained at the lead, scrabbling with his feet on the gravel path. Tom tugged at the lead till the little dog, his four feet slipping on the path, was brought behind Tom, though Tom did not achieve it at the first pull. "My goodness, he's tough!" he panted.

The farmer grinned, "Aye, he'll need to be if he's to run the hills. Have patience, lad. He'll learn in time."

At last Tom manœuvred Flash behind him.

"Now, Tom, every time he tries to pass in front of you, wave the stick from side to side before him."

"So that's what the stick's for?" Tom remarked.

"Aye, but keep giving him the word of command too."

"Come behind, Flash!" Tom kept repeating, waving the stick like a sorcerer making an incantation over a cauldron. Flash looked bewildered as he followed the movement of the stick from side to side, but he made no attempt to break away.

"Not so fast, lad! You'll have him mesmerized," John Meggetson chuckled. "Now try taking a few steps and see if he'll follow you."

Still moving the stick, Tom gave a little tug to the lead, saying loudly, "Come behind, Flash!" Flash bounded forward to the right but the waving stick warned him back. He darted to the left but again the stick was there. After several more ineffectual attempts to get round, he gave it up and meekly followed behind Tom.

"He's learning," Uncle John approved. "Now, keep him at that for ten minutes at a time, twice a day, no more."

"What do I teach him next?" Tom asked eagerly.

"Nothing, lad. One thing at a time till he's mastered it." Tom's face fell.

"You see, Tom, a pup's like a child. He can only stand so much teaching at a time. Short lessons of ten minutes repeated twice a day and he'll learn fast enough," Uncle John explained. "Don't confuse him with too much to begin with."

"All right," Tom agreed, but he still looked a bit disappointed.

"When's he's finished his lesson you can give him a pat on his head and say he's a good dog. That'll give him confidence, but no chocolate cake, mind!" There was a twinkle in Uncle John's eye. "You can take him off the lead now and let him have a good free scamper in the paddock. I must awa' to the sheep."

John Meggetson summoned Jeff with a whistle and set off at a steady pace towards the nearest hill while Tom continued the lesson with lead and stick. Before the end of the time the little dog seemed to grasp what was required of him. He made fewer darts to elude the stick and began to trot obediently behind Tom. At the end of the lesson Tom stooped and patted the dog on the head. "Good dog, Flash!"

In delight Flash rolled over on his back, waving all four paws in the air. Tom took the lead off him and in a second Flash was on his feet and capering madly about Tom, leaping in joy at his freedom again. Tom let the little dog run round the paddock for a while, then he turned towards the gate. The dog followed him. "Come behind, Flash!" he cried, waving the stick. The dog retreated a step or two and fell in behind.

"I do believe you'd follow me of your own accord if I let you out through the gate," Tom said aloud.

"Not yet, Tom! You've not had him long enough. He's got to learn obedience first." It was Aunt Jane speaking. She had come out to see how the lesson was going. "If he got loose he might run away to the hills and goodness knows when you'd see him again."

Flash went scampering after a bumble bee and Tom took the chance to nip through the gate and close it. The little dog stood forlornly at the end of the paddock.

"Watch this, Aunt Jane!" Tom cried. "Flash! Flash!"

The dog came bounding towards him.

"Guid sakes! He knows his name already," Aunt Jane exclaimed. "He'll be a wonder dog, that one!" But she was not looking at the dog but at Tom, a different, transfigured Tom from the unhappy silent boy who had come to them at first.

Uncle John insisted that only Tom should feed Flash and when, each evening, Tom put down the dish of meat for the dog and called his name, the dog appeared instantly.

"Aye, he's learned his name and to come to you now," Uncle John remarked when Flash ran up without hesitation. "The next lesson we'll take him off the lead, but you must still keep the stick to direct him and give him the usual command, 'Come behind!' Always use the same words, so the dog gets used to them."

After making a round or two of the paddock Tom slipped off the lead and cried, "Come behind, Flash!" For a moment Flash seemed surprised at the lack of the restraining lead, then by newly acquired habit he fell in at Tom's heels and trotted solemnly round the paddock, keeping a wary eye on the stick which warned him not to venture too far in front.

"Grand! Grand!" Meggetson commented. "He's learned his first lesson weel."

"Can I take him out for a walk now without the lead, Uncle John?"

The farmer shook his head. "Not yet."

"But *you* said he'd learned his lesson," Tom protested, slightly rebellious.

"Aye, but he's got other lessons to learn first. There are far ower many sheep on those hills to let him loose yet. It he gets running wild among them, scattering them he'll always want to *chase* sheep, not herd them."

"What lesson next, then?" Tom asked.

"He's got to learn to lie down on his stomach at the word 'Down!' Then, if he's working wi' sheep, you've got control over him."

Tom looked perplexed. "How do I teach him that?"

"Put the lead on him again."

Tom snapped the lead on Flash's collar.

"Now press downward on his collar, saying 'Down!' quite clearly as you do so."

Tom gently forced the little dog into a crouching position saying "Down!" in a loud voice. Surprised, Flash obeyed, but immediately tried to rise again. Tom repeated the pressure again and again.

"Now pat him on the head when he does stay down of his own accord," Uncle John instructed.

At about the twentieth try Flash seemed to get the notion of what was wanted and stayed crouching at Tom's feet. Tom patted him affectionately and praised him and Flash shot out his tongue and licked Tom's hand.

"Practise 'Come behind' and 'Down' several times a day, Tom, off the lead in the paddock, but until he has learned absolute obedience you mustn't let him off the lead outside the paddock."

"Can I take him for a walk *on* the lead?" Tom asked.

"Aye, ye might do that, but take the stick and see he keeps behind ye. Go down the farm road by the river and keep him well away from the sheep. We'll introduce him to them later on."

"Can't I *run* him on the lead?"

Uncle John smiled. "A bit of exercise'll be good for both of you. The minute you slow down to a walk, though, see he jogs *behind* you. That's his place and he's got to know it."

Tom and Flash scampered down to the river. Mrs. Meggetson came to the gate. She shaded her eyes against the setting sun and watched the pair of them.

"He's a different laddie since that dog came to the farm,"

she pronounced. "Flash seems to have given him a kind of purpose."

"Does he help you round the farm as he promised to do?"

"Oh, aye! He took a hand at scrubbing out the hen-houses today without being asked. I shall miss him when he goes to school."

"School? That's another problem." Uncle John frowned a little. "I doubt if Tom's going to take kindly to school if he has to leave Flash behind at the farm."

"There's a week or two yet till the school opens," Aunt Jane said easily.

When Flash had thoroughly mastered his two lessons and was quick to obey the words "Come behind!" and "Down!", Uncle John said, "Now it's time he got used to the sheep. We'll try him loose in the farm-yard first, though, with the gates shut." There was a twinkle in his eyes.

Tom made sure the gates on the steading were closed before he slipped the lead from Flash's neck. He wondered how his uncle would try out Flash without any sheep present. Just then a number of ducks began to waddle in procession across the farm-yard to a small pond. Flash flew at them, barking. The ducks scattered, quacking angrily.

Horrified Tom yelled at the top of his voice, "Down, Flash! Down!" fearful of his uncle's wrath.

Flash hesitated, looked desperately at the ducks, then stopped in the middle of his run and crouched low, growling a little. The ducks huddled together in a corner of the farm-yard and stood there, lifting one flat webbed foot and then another, letting out indignant quacks. Flash, his head raised between his forepaws, never took his eyes off them. They seemed to be mesmerized by him.

"I'm sorry, Uncle John! I'd forgotten about the ducks when I let him off the lead," Tom apologized.

"I hadn't!" Mr. Meggetson said. Tom was surprised to find his uncle chuckling. "I wanted to see how Flash would go on with the ducks. Look at him with his eyes fixed on them! That dog's got the eye all right!"

"The eye?" Tom looked puzzled. "What do you mean?"

"It's a power some sheep-dogs have, Tom, the power to hold the sheep in one place just by staring at them. They don't all have it, but the dogs that do, they make the champions."

"And Flash has it?"

"Look at him, lad! The ducks darena' stir from the corner for his eye being fixed on them."

Tom could hardly hide his delight at this information.

"Call him off now and see if he'll come at your bidding," his uncle suggested.

"Flash! Flash! Come behind!" Tom cried in his most commanding voice.

Somewhat reluctantly Flash rose to his feet and took his eyes off the ducks. He trotted obediently to Tom who pointed to the ground at his feet and said "Down!" Flash obeyed and Tom stooped and patted him.

As if released from a magic spell the ducks began waddling quickly towards the pond, fluttering their wings now and again to quicken their pace. Only when they were safely floating on the surface of the pond did they quack defiance at Flash.

"Aye, the dog's learned obedience to your command," Uncle John commented. "For such a young dog he's shaping very weel indeed. You can let him herd the ducks to the water now and again. It'll be fun for both o' you, but be sure that he doesna take hold o' the ducks wi' his mouth, or your aunt'll no' be sparing wi' her tongue on either of us."

Tom and his uncle grinned at each other. It was as though they had entered into a secret alliance.

"Wait a wee while and we'll try Flash wi' a few sheep," Uncle John promised.

The summer days wore on and though Tom sometimes sighed for his beloved Thames and the teeming crowds of London, the longing to go back became less intense whenever he looked at the little black dog with the white chest and muzzle and the white tip to his tail. Flash would not be parted from Tom and followed him everywhere. Soon Tom was able to take him for walks without putting on the lead, though he still did not take him among the flocks of sheep on the rounded green hillsides.

"When Tom goes to school that dog's going to be miserable without him," Aunt Jane predicted.

"Aye, there'll be a bit o' bother wi' the pair o' them, I'm thinking," Uncle John surmised. "Maybe I should have a word with Mr. Donaldson, the schoolmaster, about the lad?"

"That would be a good idea," Aunt Jane agreed.

A letter arrived for Tom from Kate in America. She wrote about her wedding and her new home.

"Hymer managed to get an apartment for us. It is a nice small flat with a living room, a kitchen, bathroom and one bedroom. He couldn't get anything bigger though he tried. I'm sorry, Tom, that we can't get you over here yet awhile till we have a bigger place with two bedrooms. Apartments are hard to find in the city. If something turns up, though, Hymer says you can come then. In the meantime I hope you are settling down well at Birkhope and that Aunt and Uncle will not mind having you for a while longer."

Tom's face set hard when he read the letter, but he passed it to Aunt Jane without a word and rose abruptly from the table. He went down to the river and called Flash to follow him. He stood moodily throwing pebbles into the water. It was plain Kate did not really want him. He wondered if she ever would do so and whether his uncle and aunt would get tired of him staying at Birkhope? Flash looked up anxiously into his face and whined. Suddenly Tom stooped and put his arms about the little dog. "Whatever happens I'll have *you*!" he declared fiercely. "No one is going to take you away from me. You're all that really *belongs* to me."

When he got back to the farmhouse neither Aunt Jane nor Uncle John made any comment on the letter, though that night at supper, Aunt Jane put an extra large piece of apple pie on his plate and Uncle John asked Tom if he'd like to walk up the hill and look at the sheep with him after supper and take Flash too. On the way he talked to the boy about Flash, as if anxious to take his mind off the letter.

"It seems a good chance to introduce Flash to the sheep," he said, "but ye'll need to keep him on the lead yet till he's got used to them. It wouldna' do for him to go after them like he went after the ducks."

When they reached the first small flock on the hill Tom said "Come behind!" very sternly and Flash obeyed, eyeing the sheep between Tom's leg and the poised stick.

"Walk Flash on the lead round the sheep and let him have a good look at them," John Meggetson instructed Tom.

The puppy quivered and strained a little at the lead but Tom held fast and walked him several times round the sheep bunched together on the hillside. As they moved round, the sheep kept moving round too, keeping their heads to the dog, watching him warily but not trying to break away. Flash never took his eyes off them.

"What did I tell you? Yon dog has got the power of the eye," Uncle John said with satisfaction. "You can take him a bit closer to them, but dinna' let him run *at* the sheep."

Tom went closer in several times and Flash behaved well, walking behind him sedately on the lead.

"That's grand," Uncle John approved. "Tomorrow we'll start him learning to drive a few sheep in the paddock."

Somehow, when Tom went to bed that night, Kate's letter did not seem to matter so much and he thought far more about the way Flash had reacted to the sheep.

Next day Uncle John had a few sheep placed in the small field known as the paddock which was next to the house.

"Keep the lead on Flash yet, but let him drive the sheep bit by bit into the corner of the paddock. Make him go down on his stomach every few steps so that he does not frighten the sheep but moves them along quietly."

Tom led Flash towards the sheep. The dog, still on the lead, ran forward two or three yards. The sheep began to move away towards the corner, then Tom cried, "Down!" In an instant the puppy was crouching on his stomach, his eyes glaring at the sheep. The sheep stood still, watching him. Another move towards them and they bunched towards the corner. At each move of a few yards Tom ordered Flash to go down and the little dog obeyed, though once or twice it was rather reluctantly, as though he would like to hurry up the job. At last the sheep were penned in in the corner.

"Weel done!" Uncle John said. "Now take the lead off him, Tom, but tell him to stay down and we'll see what happens."

Tom bent down and released the dog, pushing Flash's head down as he did so and saying "Down!" Like a miracle Flash obeyed!

For a couple of minutes neither sheep nor dog stirred, Flash holding them by his steadfast stare, then Tom put the lead on him again and the spell was broken. Flash gave a burst of barking and strained at the lead.

"Quiet, lad!" the farmer said. "Quiet, Flash! The best sheepdogs dinna' bark unless they want to call the master's attention."

With a final bark and growl Flash settled down.

"That's shown Flash the power he has over the sheep. No' bad! No' bad!" From John Meggetson "No' bad!" was the highest praise. "Ye've to keep at that drill now, Tom, for two or three weeks till Flash is quite sure what is required of him. I'll leave a few sheep in the paddock every day but ye must never let him run at them and scatter them."

Through the warm summer days the training went on and Tom and the dog became more and more absorbed in each other. Out on the hills the green grass took a tawny tinge and the heather buds appeared.

"Ye'd think that dog knew what the lad was *thinking*. Tom scarcely needs to say a word to him," Aunt Jane remarked one evening when Tom was out for a walk with Flash.

"Aye, the lad's done far better than ever I thought he would," Uncle John agreed. "Mind, though, he's got the best o' material to work on in Flash. That dog comes of the best strain of Border collies."

"All the same the boy should have some companionship besides a dog and two old folk like us," Aunt Jane said thoughtfully.

"Weel, the time's getting near for the school to take up." Uncle John sounded not altogether pleased with the thought himself.

"True enough. It might not be a bad idea if Tom got to know one or two of the other pupils before he goes to the school. He's like a kind of foreigner, ye know, and he might feel strange with the other children at first and they'd feel strange with him."

"What can *we* do about it?"

"Perhaps you should take Tom to see Mr. Donaldson the schoolmaster. There's the minister's laddie, too. He goes to the school. Maybe Tom might get to know him."

"They're all a fair step away," Uncle John pointed out.

"Have ye no' got a car, man?" Aunt Jane asked impatiently.

"Ye're surely never meaning I should take the car out just to go round visiting folk?" Uncle John sounded incredulous.

"I am indeed!"

"Guid sakes, wumman! Ye'll have us calling like the gentry yet!"

"Look here, John Meggetson!" His wife pointed her knitting needle at him. "I'm a patient woman but there are times when even I could get up and shake you. Maybe *I'd* like to see a bit of company too."

"But there's many a day when you go to the Friday Market at Peebles wi' me and you get a turn round the shops then. Oh, aye, and Mistress Bain from Cairnwold Farm picks you up in her car on Tuesdays to go to the Women's Guild," John Meggetson expostulated.

"Aye, in Mistress Bain's *own* car!" Aunt Jane sounded ominous. "There are times when I think I'll get a car o' my own."

"Michty me, Jane!" John exclaimed, almost bereft of speech.

"What for'no'?" Jane Meggetson demanded. "Can ye give me a good reason?"

"Weel, we've got a car already."

"Aye, and a grand lot of use it is to me when ye canna' even take me out in it whiles of an evening," Jane said reproachfully.

John Meggetson put on a resigned expression. "I can see

there's no help for it. Which is it to be, the minister or the schoolmaster?"

"The minister first and we'll go tomorrow night!" Jane replied with instant decision.

The next evening supper was earlier than the usual hour of seven o'clock and Aunt Jane appeared in a floral patterned silk dress. John Meggetson eyed her with apprehension.

"You're awful smart the night!"

"Aye," Aunt Jane said shortly. "And I'll thank you to take off yon baggy suit you wear among the sheep and put on your best blue one."

"My church-going suit?" Uncle John sounded horrified.

"Aye, it's time it had an airing," Aunt Jane said briskly. "And you, Tom, get into your best pullover and clean your shoes and give your face a good wash."

Uncle John pulled a face at Tom behind Aunt Jane's back and with the air of a conspirator he announced, "But we'd thought o' giving Flash a turn on the hill."

"Ah, weel, maybe you should think again," Aunt Jane told him with the calm air of a woman who has made up her mind. "Either we go visiting the minister or the school-master the night or I draw my Egg Savings out o' Peebles Post Office and buy a car!"

Tom looked up with interest. "What kind of a car, Aunt Jane? A Jaguar?"

"Mebbe!" Aunt Jane replied recklessly, hardly knowing one make of car from another. The light of battle was in her eye.

"It's a right expensive car," John said hastily.

"Mm, weel, I daresay I've got a nice bit of money put by from the sale o' the eggs and poultry this many a year and I havena' spent any of it," Aunt Jane remarked with the casual air of one who could order a fleet of Jaguars without flicking an eyelid. "Ye'd better get into that blue suit or I might even be thinking of a Rolls Royce." This was a car of which she *had* heard.

John Meggetson knew when he was bested and he went meekly upstairs to change into his blue suit. When he and Tom returned to the farm kitchen it was in their Sunday best and with faces scrubbed.

"That's better!" Aunt Jane said, eyeing them appraisingly. Flash jumped up from his favourite place on the hearth-rug, expecting to be taken for a walk.

"Shall we be able to take Flash?" Tom asked.

Aunt Jane hesitated. "Weel, mebbe no', Tom. Both the schoolmaster and the minister have got dogs and it might no' do to put Flash with them. Puppies can sometimes be impudent to older dogs and the older dogs resent it."

Tom looked disappointed but he realized the wisdom of his aunt's decision.

"Weel, seeing it's got to be, let's get going!" Uncle John said, looking as if he wanted to get over an unpleasant visit to the dentist. He took his tweed cap from a peg behind the door.

"John Meggetson! Ye'll no' be thinking of going visiting in that dirty old greasy cap?" Aunt Jane exclaimed. "The minister would be black affronted. Go get your trilby!"

"I may as weel be hung for a sheep as for a lamb!" Uncle John remarked resignedly as he hung the cap back on its peg and brought his trilby from the hall-stand. Flash began to follow them hopefully.

"No! Back, Flash!" Tom commanded. The puppy stopped, lifting first one foreleg and then the other and finally, with a melancholy eye, returned to the hearthrug. The three went out to the waiting car, Uncle John banging the kitchen door as they left. None of them knew the tweed cap had been jerked from its peg and fallen to the floor!

4 THREE VISITS AND A TWEED CAP

THE CAR ROLLED along towards Peebles and the manse where the minister, Mr. Campbell, lived. Aunt Jane sat up very straight, looking from right to left with satisfaction, ready to bow to her acquaintances. They drew up at the manse door and got out.

"Ring the bell, John!" Aunt Jane ordered. It was obviously not the correct thing for her to ring the bell for herself. After a look of surprise John Meggetson obeyed.

As the jingling died away an elderly woman appeared at the door. It was Mrs. Murray, the minister's housekeeper with whom Aunt Jane was only slightly acquainted. Mrs. Murray seemed surprised to see the three of them on the doorstep.

"Is Mr. Campbell at home?" Mrs. Meggetson asked politely.

"No, he's in Edinburgh," the housekeeper replied.

"Mrs. Campbell then?"

"She's gone with him. What were you wanting, Mrs. Meggetson?" Mrs. Murray was nothing if not forthright.

"Well—we thought we'd like our nephew to make his acquaintance and—and his son's, as the laddies will be attending the same school."

A face peered round Mrs. Murray. It belonged to Douglas Campbell, the minister's son.

"Oh, there you are, Douglas!" Mrs. Meggetson said.

The boy made no move to come forward but just stared at Tom who stared back in his turn.

"Will ye' not come and shake hands wi' Tom?" Mrs. Meggetson said, slightly exasperated. Douglas came forward reluctantly and took Tom's hand in a limp grasp.

"Where's he come from?" he asked Mrs. Meggetson as though Tom was dumb.

Tom spoke for himself. "London!" he said proudly.

"I've heard my father say London's a dirty wicked city," the boy replied, his lips curving downward in disapproval.

"That's not true!" Tom said indignantly. "It's no worse than any other city."

"Ssh! Ssh, Tom!" Mrs. Meggetson said, taken aback. "I daresay the minister had reason for what he said."

"It's a lie!" Tom persisted. "London's a grand place with wide streets and parks. It's not dirty!"

"My father does not tell lies," Douglas Campbell said righteously.

"Then he doesn't know what he's talking about," Tom replied bluntly. "He can't have seen the Thames the Embankment and the Houses of Parliament and Westminister Bridge and—and——" A sudden wave of nostalgia for London choked him and he could say no more.

"What impudence!" the housekeeper remarked, regarding Tom dourly.

"There's no good done by standing on the step arguing about London if Mr. Campbell's no' here," Uncle John decided. "We'd be as weel to get into the car again."

"I'll thank you to tell Mr. Campbell that we called to see him," Aunt Jane told the housekeeper with dignity.

Uncle John opened the car door and they all got in. Tom looked back to see Douglas Campbell pulling a face and putting out his tongue at him. Like lightning he put out his tongue in return but he was not quick enough for Aunt Jane.

"Tom Stokes, I'm ashamed of you!" she said in annoyance.

"He shouldn't have said what he did about London," Tom replied, hot with temper.

"You shouldn't have answered him back like that, Tom," his aunt reproved him.

"What for no'?" Uncle John said unexpectedly. "There was no' call for Douglas Campbell to be making his remarks about London. He started the ball rolling, no' Tom!"

Jane Meggetson stared at him. "Douglas Campbell's the minister's son, I'll remind you."

"That doesna' matter. That's no excuse for him," Uncle John replied stubbornly. There was silence for a few minutes then he enquired, "Are you still wanting to go see the schoolmaster?"

"I don't know!" Aunt Jane said, looking put out.

"Ah, weel, there's no sense in getting all decked out in our best if we dinna' finish the job," Uncle John said, and he turned in the direction of the school-house.

They found Alexander Donaldson at home. He greeted Uncle John warmly. "Man, John Meggetson, I've got something the day that'll fairly make you open your eyes!" he said. He led the way into his book-lined sitting room. "Sit ye down while I bring it." He pulled forward an armchair for Mrs. Meggetson, then disappeared into the kitchen premises. He returned bearing a large dish in his hand.

"Look what I've got on this ashet!" he said with pride, using the Scottish word for a large meat dish. There, on the ashet, was a huge speckled trout. Uncle John gazed at it in admiration and awe.

"Man, that's a right big fish! It'll be close on four pounds."

"Four pounds one ounce!" Mr. Donaldson said with pride.

"Where did ye tak' him?"

"Ye know the pool near where the Leithen Water runs into the Tweed? I got him there. I've been after him for days."

"What fly did ye use?" Uncle John asked with all the enthusiasm of a fisherman.

"A grey hen with a rusty body," Mr. Donaldson replied.

Tom opened his eyes wide. He had never heard of anybody fishing with a grey hen! Mr. Donaldson saw his astonished look and laughed.

"It's the name of a fly, laddie. I tried him with several and I began to think he was too wise for me, but he rose at last to the grey hen."

"Did he put up a fight?" Uncle John asked.

"Aye, so he did! He had my reel whirring like a whirligig at a fair as I played him up and down the river. I thought I'd tire before he did, or else my line would snap. It took me every bit of half an hour to land him."

The two men gazed in rapt admiration at the big fish and the conversation began to drift into talk of pools and currents and fishing gear and flies. Tom sat as one listening to a foreign tongue. It all went over his head. Even Aunt Jane got restive. She cleared her throat determinedly at last.

"Aye, it's a fair wonder o' a fish," she agreed, "but you mustn't forget what we've come to see Mr. Donaldson about, John."

"Oh, aye!" Uncle John replied, as one coming to himself. "Aye, it's about the lad here, our nephew Tom. Ye'll have room for him in the school at the start o' the term?"

"Aye, there's room. Which part of the country are you from, lad?"

"London!" Tom said explosively, waiting for the derogatory remark against his city, but none came.

Mr. Donaldson looked a little surprised at the lad's tone but all he said was, "Most London schools have a good name. You should have had quite a fair degree of education there. How old are you?"

"Twelve." Tom replied briefly.

"Mm! Then you'll have passed your eleven plus exam?"

"No." Tom sounded defiant.

"But you'll have taken the exam, surely?"

Tom shook his head but vouchsafed no explanation.

"But you're of the age to have sat the exam. Were you ill at the time."

It would have been easy for Tom to say "Yes" but there was always a downright honesty in Tom that would not let him lie.

"No. I—I played truant on the day I should have been at the exam," he admitted.

"Tom Stokes!" Aunt Jane exclaimed, horrified.

Even Uncle John looked rather nonplussed. "You never told us that, lad!"

"You never asked me!" Tom gulped.

"Oh, what a shocking thing to do!" Aunt Jane said.

"At least Tom has told us quite honestly of his own accord what happened," Mr. Donaldson said quietly. "Maybe other opportunities will offer themselves yet. All is not finished if you don't get the eleven plus at the right age. Is Tom likely to be staying with you for a length of time, Mr. Meggetson?"

Mr. and Mrs. Meggetson looked rather helplessly at each other.

"It's this way, Mr. Donaldson," Mrs. Meggetson began. "Tom's sister has gone to America to be married, and she hasn't been able to make arrangements for Tom to go out to her, so he may be here quite a while."

Tom's eyes burned with bitterness. "Her last letter said they'd got a nice apartment but they'd got no room in it for me. I don't think her husband wants me there," he blurted out.

"Give her time, Tom. It may not be easy for them," Aunt Jane said quietly.

Tom shook his head unhappily.

Mr. Donaldson gave him a keen glance. "What did you do in your spare time when you were not at school, Tom? Did you belong to any boys' clubs?"

Tom shook his head. "No. I just used to go round with other lads looking at things, you know."

"What kind of things?" Mr. Donaldson persisted.

"Oh, I dunno!" Tom seemed reluctant to say. "Cars— and people and—and the ships on the river." It was as though the last was dragged out of him.

"The Thames?"

"Yes."

"There's a lot to be seen on the Thames. It's like a gateway to London," Mr. Donaldson remarked.

Tom's eye kindled gratefully for a minute, then the spark died again.

"You'll take a cup of tea now, Mrs. Meggetson?" the schoolmaster offered, but Aunt Jane had already risen to her feet.

"That's kind of you, Mr. Donaldson, but we've got another visit to make on the way home so maybe you'll forgive us."

John Meggetson eyed the big trout reluctantly. He would have liked to stay and talk fishing with Alexander Donaldson.

"My! That's the bonniest trout I've seen this many a day," he said as he followed his wife out of the room.

They said goodbye and the car started off once more.

"What was your hurry?" John Meggetson asked his wife. "Are you going somewhere else?"

"You can call at the roadman's house on the way back It's no' far out of your way."

"The roadman? What are ye wanting wi' Jim Young? Are we all dressed up to go and see the roadman?" There was a hint of sarcasm in John Meggetson's voice.

"Don't talk so foolish!" Aunt Jane said, rather nettled. "I want to see Alison, his wife. She's not been well this while past since she broke her leg that bad winter. She was a good lassie to me when she helped at the farm before she was married, when our children were young."

Uncle John took the road that led to the roadman's cottage.

"Don't be too long," he said, as he stopped the car. "Tom will want to give Flash a turn outside before it's dark."

Tom threw his uncle a grateful glance.

A small dark girl opened the door to them. She had an an elf-like face with bright eyes and seemed about the same age as Tom.

"Hullo, Elspeth! I've just called to ask for your mother," Mrs. Meggetson greeted her.

"Come in, please, Mrs. Meggetson." Elspeth led the way into a tidy bright living-room. Mrs. Young sat in an easy chair, her leg stretched out on a footstool and a pile of mending beside her. A quiet-mannered, weather-beaten man rose to greet them. He was Jim Young.

"Why, it's you, Mrs. Meggetson!" Mrs. Young exclaimed with delighted welcome. "I'm sorry I canna' get up so easily."

"Dinna' try, my lassie! How's the leg?"

A cloud passed over Alison Young's face. "The bone's no' healed as it should have done. It's left one leg shorter than the other and I canna' walk without pain."

"How are you managing, then, Alison?"

"Elspeth's a good lassie about the house and Jim helps her. I can do sitting-down jobs like preparing the food and even the ironing."

"Are the doctors not doing anything for it?"

"Doctor McAulay wants her to go to the hospital in Edinburgh to have it re-set. Ye see, the damage was done to it when she had to lie so long when it was broken and the doctor couldna' get up the valley for the snow drifts," Jim Young explained.

"When will you be going to the hospital then?" Mrs. Meggetson asked.

"I canna' say! It's kind o' difficult. I don't like to leave Elspeth on her own and sometimes, when Jim's been working at a distance, it's been awful late when he's got back. She's such a bit lassie and it's so lonely here. Anything might happen."

"Mm!" Mrs. Meggetson looked thoughtful.

All this time Elspeth had been quietly busy putting the kettle on the fire and setting cups and saucers on a tray. Tom, slightly bored and aching to get back to Flash, watched her as she moved about. Shyly she proffered cake along with the welcome cup of tea.

"This cake's very good, Alison. Ye've no' lost your light hand with a sponge," Mrs. Meggetson remarked.

"Oh, Elspeth made that," Mrs. Young said.

"Weel done, lassie!" Mr. Meggetson approved.

Elspeth blushed and went away to fill up the kettle again.

When they had finished their tea Mrs. Meggetson said rather pointedly, "Will you take Tom to see your

rabbits, Elspeth, while I have a bit talk with your mother?"

Elspeth led the way to an outhouse behind the cottage where some of the road-repairing tools were stored. Standing against its wall was a well-constructed rabbit hutch in which were two silky Angora rabbits and several tiny ones that looked like small balls of fluff. Tom looked at them with interest.

"That's Bill and Betty and their family," Elspeth told him shyly.

"My! They're fine rabbits!" Tom exclaimed.

"Aye, they're right bonnie, aren't they?" Elspeth was pleased with Tom's admiration. She opened the hutch. "Like to lift one out? Go on! Betty won't mind. She's used to me handling her babies."

Tom lifted out one silky-coated little creature and stroked it.

"Have you any rabbits?" Elspeth asked him.

"No, but I've got a dog up at the farm."

"What kind?"

"A sheep dog. I'm training him myself. Uncle John is showing me how to do it. He thinks Flash is going to be good." Before Tom realized it he had launched into a description of the way he was training his dog. Elspeth listened with close attention, asking a question now and again which showed she was wise in the way of sheep dogs.

"Do you like being at Birkhope, Tom?" she asked.

Tom puckered his brows. "I like it well enough when I'm out with Flash, but—but it's awfully lonely up there." He suddenly felt an urge to confide in Elspeth. "I tried to run away once."

"Whatever for? Mrs. Meggetson's real kind, isn't she?"

"Oh, yes! They're both kind. I miss London, though, the friends I used to go about with, and—and the river."

Elspeth regarded him seriously. "You ought to give the place more of a trial. You'll be going to school here and maybe you'll make some friends. It's daft to run away before you've tried to do something about it yourself."

Tom might have been resentful of such a remark but Elspeth looked so kindly at him that he could not take offence. Suddenly he asked, "Do you go to school here?"

"Yes."

"Which school?"

"Mr. Donaldson's school."

"That's where I'm to go." Tom's face brightened and the two children smiled at each other.

Aunt Jane called from the house. "Come along, Tom. We're ready to go now."

Tom thrust the little bundle of fur carefully back inside the hutch and Elspeth secured the catch.

Aunt Jane buttoned her coat. "Weel, that's all settled then, Alison," she was saying with satisfaction.

"It's very good of you, Mrs. Meggetson."

"Not a bit! You'll let me know when you get word from the hospital?"

"I'll do that, thank you."

The good-nights were said and the Meggetsons got back into the car.

"See you at the school, Elspeth!" Tom called through the window as they drove away.

When they reached the farm Flash greeted them with a "Wuff" of welcome that sounded as though he was very pleased with himself.

"What on earth's that he's got between his paws?" Uncle John asked. "Is it a rat?"

"Guid sakes, I hope not! Not in my kitchen!" Aunt Jane cried in alarm. She took a nearer look. "Mercy on us! If it's not your old cap! It must have fallen off the peg when you closed the door."

Mr. Meggetson snatched up the cap, hardly recognizable as a cap any more. Flash had chewed it to ribbons!

"Weel, it only wanted that to complete the evening!" he declared, looking ruefully at the remains.

When Tom saw his uncle's look he felt a sudden anger at Flash.

"You bad dog!" he said, lifting his hand to smack the puppy. Uncle John caught him by the elbow.

"No, no, Tom! You must never lift your hand to the dog in anger. He's but a pup and *he* thinks he's done something clever. To him that cap was an *enemy* to be worried. *You* must teach him better."

"How?" Tom asked.

"That I'm going to leave you to work out for yourself, lad. It's a thought late to be starting on Flash's next lesson tonight. There's always tomorrow."

Tom had kept Flash at his drill in the paddock with three sheep till he was well disciplined and did not run at them to scatter them. He crouched at Tom's command and held the sheep by the power of his eye.

"Aye, he's ready now to make a cast," Uncle John decided.

"A cast? What's that?"

"He's got to run in a wide half-circle round the sheep to the back of them, to right or left at the word of command, and bring the flock in gradually towards you. We'll take him out on the hillside with the same three sheep. He'll have more room to run there. Jeff can take them along for us, but once we've reached the pasture, then Flash can take over."

Uncle John whistled up Jeff and, with Flash on the lead, they took the sheep up the hillside. Though Flash trotted obediently behind Tom he watched Jeff jealously and now and again gave a little whine of impatience and even annoyance.

"We'll have to change these sheep, Tom. Flash is beginning to look upon them as his property and that won't do," Uncle John decided. "Besides, the sheep are beginning to know what's expected of them and to obey the commands too."

"Are sheep really as clever as that?" Tom asked in surprise.

"Sheep are no' as stupid as some folk would have you believe. True, they follow each other in herds but that's a natural kind o' thing, when a crowd is a protection against their enemies."

"I've never thought of it that way," Tom confessed. "What enemies do sheep have?"

"Foxes, Tom! They go for the young lambs, aye, and carrion crows that swoop and pick out the lambs' eyes."

Tom gave a shudder.

"You should see a ewe stand up for her young then. She'll fight with her little stumps o' horns if she's driven to it and lash out with her hoofs. Here we are in the field. Come awa' to me, Jeff!" Uncle John shouted, giving a shrill whistle with his fingers to his mouth. Obediently Jeff left the sheep and came trotting back to his master.

"It's all Flash's now," Uncle John said. "Take the stick, Tom, and point firmly away to your right and send him *round* the sheep. At the same time shout "Awa' here!" to him in a loud voice.

Tom slipped the lead from Flash and did as Uncle John told him, pointing with the stick to his right and shouting in a clear voice "Away here, Flash!"

Flash looked at him uncertainly for a moment, then set off running in the direction to which Tom pointed, then he faltered, looked round and stood, not knowing quite what to do.

"Why doesn't he go on?" Tom cried in a disappointed voice.

"Here's where you've got to be patient, Tom. This is the first really *hard* lesson Flash has had to learn. Call him back to you and begin all over again. This time let him look at the sheep first, then point your stick to the right and make a circling movement with it to show him you want him to come in behind the sheep. Ye'll maybe have to do it as many as twenty or thirty times before he gets the idea, but call him straight back and begin over again every time he goes wrong. Be stern with him at the same time to let him know ye're not pleased."

All at once, after half-a-dozen tries, Flash seemed to grasp what Tom meant him to do and he ran in a wide half-circle round the little flock and behind them. It was Uncle John's turn to get excited.

"Fine! Fine! A good turn of speed and he's coming in nicely behind them at a fair distance. Tell him to drop down. Quick, Tom!"

"Down! Down, Flash!" Tom bellowed at the top of his voice.

Astonished, but obedient, Flash flopped down reluctantly.

"Grand! Just grand!" Uncle John approved. "Look! The sheep have faced round to him and he's holding them by the power of his eye."

"What do we do now?" Tom asked, eager to continue.

"Steady, lad, steady, or the dog will catch your impatience! Now you've to make him bring the sheep towards you very slowly, driving them like he did in the paddock. Whistle him up. Then, after a few yards, make him go down and wait for your next command."

Tom gave a whistle and in an instant Flash was up and the sheep turned and galloped before him. Before Flash came near them Tom shouted "Down!" and Flash stopped and crouched on his stomach again, though he went down with a look of frustration. The sheep trotted on a few yards then stopped and faced round. They did not seem unduly alarmed by Flash's movements, but when he fixed them with his eye, they seemed to freeze where they stood.

"Now make him lift the sheep again, Tom."

Tom went once more through the commands. Flash obeyed, bringing in the sheep nearer. At last the sheep were within a stone's throw of Tom and his uncle.

"Now for the last drive, Tom!"

Tom whistled and Flash sprang to life. This time, however, he was not to be denied the fun of driving the sheep as hard and far as he could. They went scampering past Tom with Flash at their heels, threatening to nip them, though he never did it!

"That's spoiled a good performance," Uncle John said ruefully. "But at least he didna' bite them!"

Tom whistled for Flash who came to him wagging his tail as though he had done something very clever.

"No, no, Flash!" Uncle John said, shaking his head at him.

"Bad dog, Flash!" Tom scolded him.

The little dog looked from one to the other, aware of their disapproval, but puzzled, as Tom slipped on the lead again.

"What do I do now, Uncle John?" Tom asked in a disappointed voice.

"Begin again, lad. It's the only way. But this time ye mustn't let Flash bring them down the whole length of the field. Stop him after a couple of 'lifts' of the sheep, then call him off and praise him when he stops. We expected too much of him the first time. Wait! I'll send Jeff to take the sheep up again'"

All this time Jeff had been watching Flash's performance, almost with a sniffy air of condescension. When he was sent to fetch the sheep back he gave a whisk of his tail as much as to say, "Watch this!" With perfect discipline, hardly even needing his master's whistle, he took the sheep up the field again to where they had been. As he came back to his master he gave Flash a sly look out of the corner of his eye.

"Showing off he is a bit!" Uncle John chuckled. "Wait! Jeff's a good dog. It'll do Flash no harm to watch his way of working. I'll send Jeff to bring the sheep down again."

Almost with an air of boredom Jeff lifted the sheep and brought them down the hill. He crouched behind them every few yards giving them a chance to stand for a few seconds, then, without hustling them, brought them to a standstill a few feet from his master.

Flash watched his performance, at first straining at the lead as if anxious to join Jeff, but when Tom said "Down!" Flash lay at his feet, panting a little and with his pink tongue flicking in and out. He kept his eye on every movement that Jeff made and when Meggetson praised his dog, Flash pricked up his ears. Meggetson made Jeff take the sheep out to the centre of the pasture again, then whistled for him to return. There was no doubt Jeff came back with a slight swagger.

"Now send Flash to fetch the sheep in towards us again," Uncle John directed.

"Away here!" Tom shouted, waving his stick to the right and then in a circle towards the sheep. Flash ran out in a wide arc to come in behind them.

"That was a perfect cast!" Uncle John said almost under his breath. "Now, down wi' him, Tom!"

"Down, Flash!" Tom commanded in ringing tones, and Flash stopped dead in his tracks and dropped to earth.

"Grand! Grand!" Uncle John muttered. "Let him lift the sheep twice and stop twice, then go and fetch him in yourself, Tom."

The puppy executed the manœuvres much as he had seen Jeff do them, then remained crouched, his eye never leaving the sheep.

"Go put the lead on him now, Tom, but praise him as you do it."

There was almost a question in Flash's eye as Tom came up to him. Was he to be praised or blamed? When Tom patted him and said "Good dog! Well done, Flash!" the little dog leaped up with delight, jumping at Tom and licking his hands.

"Quiet, boy!" Tom said, and at a wave of the stick Flash fell in behind him as they went down the field. When they reached Jeff beside Meggetson, Flash gave a short "Wuff!" of triumph, as if to say "I can do it too!"

"Shall we teach Flash to go out on the left now, Uncle John?" Tom had seen his uncle sending Jeff out both to the right and the left and he was eager for Flash to make progress.

"No, Tom. Let him have a few more lessons on the right cast and the lift and the drive first. When he's mastered that, then we can do it all again from the left cast."

"How long will it take Flash to learn the right- and left-hand commands properly?" Tom asked.

"It might take three months till he's absolutely certain of them but Flash is an intelligent wee dog and he might learn in less time than that. We'll give him a lesson morning and evening, and if you've time mid-day, there might be no harm in giving him a short lesson then too. You can give him a walk among the flocks on the hills too, Tom, but the minute he shows any sign of trying to chase them, you must put the lead on him. He must only drive them when you give him the commands."

"It takes a long time to train a sheep dog, doesn't it?" Tom commented.

"Not wearying, are you, lad?"

Tom shook his head vigorously.

At the end of that week Tom said rather proudly to his

uncle, "Flash has learned another new trick. Would you like to see it?"

They had just finished supper but Uncle John got up and reached for his stick.

"No, you don't need to go out, Uncle John! He's learned it here in the kitchen." A look of conspiracy passed between Tom and his aunt. Mrs. Meggetson produced her husband's battered and chewed cap out of a drawer. Tom tossed it in front of Flash.

"Watch it, Flash!"

Flash took up a crouching attitude, growled softly at the old cap and fixed his eyes on it but he did not attempt to touch it. Uncle John's eyes widened.

"Now, both of you come for a stroll round the garden, please," Tom said. "Will you close the kitchen door behind you, Uncle John?"

They took a turn as far as the river, then came back. Cautiously Uncle John opened the kitchen door and peered round it. Flash was still mounting guard over the old cap but not attempting to touch it.

"Make as though you're going to lift it, Uncle John."

John Meggetson pretended to make a snatch at the cap and Flash growled and bared his teeth.

"Now, see this!" Tom said. He held out his hand. "Bring it to me, Flash!"

Flash lifted the cap gingerly between his teeth and brought it to Tom.

"Weel, I'm fair dumbfoundered!" Uncle John exclaimed. "You've got him right under control, laddie."

"I'd trust that dog to watch my best hat!" Aunt Jane declared.

"My! That's saying something!" Uncle John gave Tom a wink and Tom actually found himself returning it!

5   ADVENTURE IN THE FOG

THE WEEKS OF the long summer holiday bore on relentlessly to the time of the school opening, but by the end of it Flash had learned to run to the right on the command "Away here!" and to run left when Tom shouted "Come by!" The dog watched keenly for the direction in which Tom pointed his stick and then he swung out in a wide arc, moving with lightning speed, to drop behind the sheep at Tom's command. He learned also to bring the sheep down in a straight line towards Tom without flustering them.

"That was a grand outrun!" Uncle John remarked one day. "I've never seen a dog at the Trials with a better turn of speed. The next thing is to teach him to bring sheep through a gate. For that we start with two hurdles and five sheep."

"Why do we need hurdles?" Tom asked.

"They stand for the gateposts and if a dog makes a mistake it's easier to take him over the same ground again. Besides, hurdles are used in the Sheep Dog Trials and Flash must get used to them if he's to compete."

They carried the hurdles up to the centre of the field and set them up seven yards apart. The sheep were up at the top of the field. They were sheep Flash had worked with previously.

"Once he has mastered the idea that he has to drive the sheep down between the hurdles, then we'll try him with new sheep who are not used to him. He's got to learn to handle strange sheep."

"What commands do I give to make him bring the sheep between the hurdles?" Tom asked.

"Just the same as to make him go to right or left. 'Away there!' and 'Come by!' Watch which way he is driving the sheep and which way he needs to turn. He'll soon learn to run from side to side behind his flock and keep them in a bunch when he knows what is required of him."

Flash made several very creditable attempts. He soon grasped that he must bring the sheep between the hurdles, and though at first one or two of the sheep eluded him and ran round the wooden frames, Flash quickly learned to watch for the rebel and to bring him back into line.

"I'll take him up on the hills with me along with Jeff and he can watch Jeff working while you're at school," Uncle John said.

Tom's face fell. He had forgotten that the time of the school opening was so near.

"It's all right, Tom. I shan't try to work him or give him commands myself. He's got to know he's *your* dog, but it will exercise him and he can run with Jeff. They get on well together."

"It's—it's not that, Uncle John. I—I just don't want to leave Flash."

"You'll be able to give him his training morning and night just the same and at the week-ends you can come with me when I go my rounds of the flocks." Uncle John replied, but Tom still scowled at the thought of school.

It came all too soon, the day when he set off on his two-mile walk down the valley to the school in the nearest village. In his pocket he carried his lunch of bread and cheese, an apple and a home-baked scone.

Flash got up from the hearth and followed Tom to the door, eagerly anticipating a walk. Tom looked back at him miserably.

"Awa', Tom, and shut the door behind you and I'll hold Flash," Aunt Jane said, holding on to Flash's collar.

More miserable than ever Tom shut the door behind him and went off down the turf-bordered lane, kicking moodily at the small loose stones. He had gone about a mile along the road, when he heard a bark behind him and there was Flash chasing after him as though he were a strayed sheep! The little dog caught up with him, leaping about for joy.

"Oh, Flash! Flash! You ought not to have come!" Tom cried, nevertheless hugging the little black and white dog to him. "I wonder how you managed to get out?"

Mrs. Meggetson had opened the door when she went to feed the hens and Flash had seized his opportunity and dashed out. He was determined to go with Tom. His keen nose soon picked up Tom's scent and he was hot on his track. When he reached a bend in the downhill road he saw Tom, a speck in the distance and raced after him at a speed quicker than he had ever made on an outrun after the sheep. His coming posed Tom a problem.

"Now what am I going to do with you?" Tom said aloud in dismay. "If I take you back I'll be late for school and I can't take you with me." He set the dog down on the road and pointed in the direction of the farm and said, "Go back, Flash!"

Flash ran back a few steps, then because he could not or would not understand, he crouched down in the road as he might behind a flock of sheep and waited for Tom's whistle.

"Jings!" Tom said, using Uncle John's favourite expression, "If I leave you I believe you'd wait there all day!" For a minute the temptation jumped to his mind that here was a glorious chance to play truant. It was a warm sunny day. The water in the little river tinkled and splashed its way down the valley. He had his "piece" in his pocket so that they need not go hungry. They could both return to the farm at the time his aunt would expect them and no one would be any the wiser. He could make some excuse to the schoolmaster next day that he had not been well. Then, all at once, Tom had a mind-picture of Uncle John patiently instructing him how to train Flash, gladly giving him what little leisure time he had.

"It wouldn't be fair, Flash," he said aloud, as though the dog could share his reasoning. "I've got to go to the school even if it's only *not* to let Uncle John down with Mr. Donaldson. Suppose Mr. Donaldson asked him why I wasn't at school?"

Temptation urged that it might be a long time before Uncle John saw Mr. Donaldson again and the question might never be raised, but Tom put the thought from him.

"Come on, Flash!" he called, and he went down the hill with Flash at his heels.

The children were assembling in the playground when he reached the school, but the school doors were not yet open. Tom was at a loss what to do with Flash and halted at the school gate with his hand on his collar. Just then the minister's son, Douglas Campbell, spotted him.

"Hi, you! You can't bring dogs into the playground!" he shouted officiously.

Tom ignored him and entered the playground.

"Did you hear what I said? You can't bring your beastly dog in here!"

"Mind your own business!" Tom retorted.

"Who is he?" another boy asked Campbell.

"He's just a cheeky brat from London," Campbell said.

"He even had the impudence to call my father a liar because he said that London was a dirty place. He needs a lesson in manners."

Tom's temper began to rise. "Are you going to give me one?" he challenged Douglas Campbell.

"Oh, he's wanting a fight!" cried the other boy. "Give him a punch, Douglas!"

Douglas did not know quite what to do. As the minister's son he had never had to fight for his position before, but if he did not take up the London boy's challenge he knew his prestige would fall in the eyes of his class-mates. He advanced threateningly on Tom, his fists raised and Tom lifted his own in defence. Douglas aimed a blow at Tom, but Tom side-stepped and it only grazed his shoulder.

Both boys had forgotten about Flash in the heat of the moment. Flash gave a low growl and sprang to Tom's defence. He caught Douglas by the turn-up of his long trousers and held on!

"Hi! Call your dog off!" Campbell cried to Tom.

"No!" Tom yelled back. "Not till you've apologized for calling him a beastly dog."

"I shall not!" Douglas defied him.

"Hold it, Flash!" Tom shouted.

Flash took a firmer grip on Douglas's trouser, though his teeth did not penetrate the flesh. Douglas tried to shake the dog off but that only made Flash worry at the trouser leg the more. In trying to kick at the dog Douglas over-balanced and sat down suddenly on the ground but Flash still held on. A shout of laughter went up from the ring of boys: some of them had suffered in the past from Douglas's overbearing ways. But a few small girls cried out in alarm. All at once another voice was heard and Mr. Donaldson's head appeared above the crowd.

"What's going on here?" he demanded. He looked astonished to see Douglas Campbell on the ground and a small dog with his teeth fixed in the cloth of his trouser leg.

"Come off, Flash! Come here!" Tom commanded.

Flash gave a final growl and reluctantly let go and returned to Tom.

"What's all this about?" Mr. Donaldson asked sternly.

Douglas got up from the ground. "The new boy set his dog on me," he said.

"Did you do that?" Mr. Donaldson asked Tom. Tom could only shake his head.

"Then why did the dog attack Douglas Campbell?" Mr. Donaldson wanted to know.

Tom was silent but a voice from the crowd of children spoke up for him. It was Elspeth Young's.

"Please, Mr. Donaldson, Douglas Campbell hit Tom Stokes first and the dog flew at him because of that."

"Oh, and why did you hit him, Douglas?" The head-master's voice was level and quiet.

"Because he—he brought the dog into the playground when I told him to take it out and—and because he was cheeky," Douglas faltered.

"And you thought that a sufficient reason for showing a new boy violence?" Mr. Donaldson's voice was like ice. Douglas dropped his eyes and had nothing to say.

"Why did you bring your dog to school, Tom Stokes?"

"He—he followed me, sir. If I'd turned back with him I'd have been late. I—I didn't know what to do with him." Tom answered truthfully.

"I see. Well, he had better be put in my kitchen till it's time for you to go home, but understand, Tom, that it's against the rules for you to bring animals to school."

"Yes, sir."

"You must make sure he stays up at the farm in the future. Come this way." Mr. Donaldson led the way to the kitchen and Tom followed with Flash at his heels.

"He'll be all right there, Tom. At dinner-time you can slip along and see him."

"Thanks a lot, Mr. Donaldson," Tom said gratefully. He pushed Flash inside and the door was closed firmly.

Tom found that he was placed at a desk next to Elspeth. She gave him a shy smile.

"Thanks a lot, Elspeth, for speaking up for me and Flash," Tom whispered.

"Attention over there!" Mr. Donaldson said sternly and Tom fixed his eye on the map which Mr. Donaldson was unrolling.

"We will begin the geography today with a lesson on the river Thames and London," Mr. Donaldson said in a very matter-of-fact voice, but the corners of his mouth twitched a little. Tom felt a sudden warmth in his heart as he gave Mr. Donaldson all his attention.

Two or three weeks rolled by after that in a kind of routine.

Every morning Tom rose early and gave Flash his lesson in handling sheep. The dog learned to bring first a small flock and then a larger one between the hurdles. He seemed to have no difficulty now in handling the sheep, driving them steadily towards Tom without upsetting them.

"He's doing fine!" Uncle John remarked. "Before long he'll be ready to learn how to pen the sheep in a sheep-fold."

Though Flash was obedient to Uncle John, it was to Tom that he gave all his love and loyalty and it was for Tom's commands that he listened. He seemed to know which days were Saturdays when he and Tom joined Uncle John and Jeff on the hill tops with the flocks of sheep.

As Tom took his daily walk to school the colours of the landscape changed. The purple heather faded to brown but the bracken took on first a golden yellow, then a saffron shade, and finally glowing colours of dark crimson and tawny orange and fading brown. It was Nature's last glory before the winter set in. Each night the dusk came down a little earlier and Tom had to hurry to give Flash his lesson before it was too dark.

Now and again, when the market day at Peebles was a long and busy one, Uncle John would stop at the school at the close of the afternoon session and give Tom a lift home, but this only happened occasionally. In the middle of one afternoon when it was not a market day, John Meggetson's farm wagon drew up at the school. Mr. Donaldson saw him advancing across the playground and hastily set the class to some reading while he went out to speak with him.

"Something wrong, Mr. Meggetson?"

"Weel, only in a kind of a way. Could I have wee Elspeth Young out from the class to take her to her home? You see, her mother's had word by phone today to go to the hospital in Edinburgh to have her leg re-set and she's likely to be there a few weeks. The wife promised Mrs. Young she'd have the wee lassie up at the farm. Jim Young's taking his wife into Edinburgh today and she'd like to see Elspeth before she goes."

"I'll call her out," Mr. Donaldson said at once. "Do you want Tom too?"

"No. Elspeth's mother might want a talk wi' the child. Tom can come home at the usual time."

Mr. Donaldson called Elspeth out from her class. Tom wondered if her mother was not well when Elspeth did not return. Judge of his surprise when he found Elspeth helping his aunt to set the tea-table when he got back to the farm!

"Hullo!" he exclaimed, delighted to see her.

"Elspeth's coming to stay with us for a while until her mother comes out of hospital," his aunt told him. "Now, you'll do what you can to make her feel at home, Tom?"

"Of course I will!" Tom promised. It would be good to have Elspeth for company. He talked a lot about Flash to her at school and she loved to listen.

On Saturday morning Elspeth gave Aunt Jane a hand round the house while Tom did his usual chore of cleaning out the hen-house. In the afternoon Uncle John and Tom usually took Flash on the hills for his training with the sheep but this time Tom suggested something new.

"Do you think we could teach Flash to pen sheep today?" he asked.

Mr. Meggetson hesitated.

"I thought Elspeth could watch too," Tom added quickly. "You'd like to see Flash have his lesson, wouldn't you, Elspeth?"

"Yes, I would!" Elspeth said eagerly.

Mr. Meggetson gave a smile. "Come on, then! We'll take Jeff and bring five sheep down to the steading."

With the two dogs they brought down the sheep to the field beside the farm. Elspeth had already taken up her position beside the wire fencing to watch. Tom stood by the gate into the farmyard. He whistled for Flash to bring the sheep towards him. Flash seemed a bit surprised not to find Tom standing in his usual place but he brought the little flock steadily towards the gate.

Flash brought the sheep neatly up to the gate. Tom moved to the entrance to the sheep fold and held the gate open.

With a sharp "Wuff!" as if to say he knew what he was
about, Flash brought the sheep through the gate and into
the farm-yard. There they began to scatter and Flash looked
worried. He galloped round the sheep, heading them here
and there till he had got them into a compact bunch
again.

"In with them, Flash!" Tom pointed his stick at the sheep
pen.

It was as though inspiration came to Flash. He guessed
what was required of him. Though the sheep faced about
and one tried to escape, he chased it back to the others. Then,
step by step, crouching before them and glaring at them,
he turned them into the pen. Tom shut the gate quickly on
the tiny flock.

"Good dog, Flash! Well done!" Tom praised him. Flash
rolled on the ground with delight. He *knew* he had done
well and Tom was pleased with him. Elspeth added her
praise and patted him too.

"Aye, he's done weel, right enough, though he'll need
to learn to do the job more quietly and wi' less fuss,"
Uncle John qualified his praise. "But there's no doubt about
it, the dog's got intelligence above the ordinary."

"Please, I've got some chocolate drops in my pocket.
May I give him some as a reward?" Elspeth asked.

Tom hesitated. He looked at his uncle. He knew his
views about feeding sheep dogs on sweet stuff, but for once
Uncle John relented.

"Maybe just *one*." he consented.

Elspeth went forward and held out a chocolate drop in
the palm of her hand. Very gently Flash took it between his
teeth, rolled it over in his mouth, then gave a little bark
of delight. He licked Elspeth's outstretched hand all over.

"Just look at him! Isn't he friendly?" she exclaimed.

Uncle John gave a slight chuckle. "He's even licking the *smell* o' the chocolate from your hand!"

Elspeth had started something that Flash found very quick to learn. Whenever Elspeth was present when Tom finished a lesson and he praised Flash, the dog looked eagerly from Tom to Elspeth and soon it became part of the routine that when Tom said "Yes, he can have it," Elspeth gave him *one* chocolate drop.

"Maybe just one will do him no harm, but no more, mind! And you've only to give him one when he's done his lesson properly. He must know it's a reward," Uncle John made the rule.

Tom began to welcome Elspeth's quiet presence in the background when he was training Flash. The dog began to look round to see she was there, too. Perhaps the chocolate drop had something to do with it, but he seemed to try harder when Elspeth was there.

Indoors, Elspeth quickly became one of the household. Aunt Jane would find the washing-up done and the vegetables prepared and even the ironing finished and folded.

"That lassie's a treasure," she told her husband. "It'll seem queer in the house without her when she goes back home."

"Ah, weel, ye've no call to worry about that yet," John Meggetson said. "I was speaking wi' Jim Young the day. He's working on the top road above Whitecraig and he was telling me that Alison's doing fine, but it'll be a long job."

"What's Alison's loss is our gain, anyway," Aunt Jane said with philosophy. "Besides, I think Elspeth's doing Tom a power o' good. He's a different laddie from when he came here."

"I don't deny Elspeth's had a hand in it, but Flash had already started the good work," Uncle John declared.

The long walk to and from school seemed shorter in

Elspeth's company. Elspeth knew so much about the wild life of the moorlands that fringed the road; where the peewits nested and the grouse might be found; the names of the moorland flowers; where to look for sticklebacks and trout in the river. In his turn Tom told her about London and the Thames, and she listened fascinated, putting an occasional question.

It was much better, too, doing his homework alongside Elspeth and checking his results by hers.

"I doubt Mr. Donaldson would hardly approve them comparing their answers in arithmetic," Uncle John remarked drily to Aunt Jane one night.

"Och, when they get different answers, then they know *one* of them is wrong, and so they go through it again together and find where the fault is," Aunt Jane told him. "That way they're *learning*, and if that's no' what homework is for, then I'm clean daft! Mr. Donaldson's a sensible man and I'm sure he thinks like me," she finished complacently. There was no doubt, however, that Tom was taking greater interest in his school work.

One afternoon, about an hour before school usually closed, Mr. Donaldson looked through the window. One of the sudden autumnal fogs that occur among the Border Hills of Scotland was seeping along the valley and beginning to blot out the landscape.

"You may close your books and put away your exercises." the headmaster announced. "We shall finish school for this afternoon. There is a mist rising which promises to get much thicker. You are not to linger playing round the school. You must all go straight home."

There was a scurry of delight among the pupils at the unexpected early hour of liberation. In a few minutes they were all pouring out of the school gates.

Tom and Elspeth began the long trudge uphill to Birk-hope. Already the mist was beginning to spiral about them in wraith-like figures. The air was clammy and damped their clothing and made elf-locks of Elspeth's hair. Before long it was difficult even to see the opposite side of the road. The mist seemed to dance round them in dizzying specks. Elspeth peered about her. "We'd better hurry, Tom. The fog's growing thicker."

They pressed on. Only the sound of their feet on the metalled surface told them they were still on the road. Once or twice they strayed off on to the grass verges and had to cast round to find the road again. Their pace grew slower, for they were frightened of stumbling off the road and into the ditch which ran alongside.

"I don't like this at all," Elspeth said, shivering. "Surely we should have come to the cross-roads by now?"

"Cheer up, Elspeth! It can't be far away and after that we should soon reach the bridge. Once we've crossed the river there are the wire fences to Uncle John's fields to guide us." Tom spoke with more confidence than he really felt.

They stumbled on a few paces more.

"I think we're at the cross-roads now," Elspeth said. She crossed to the right hand side of the road, disappearing from sight. Suddenly she gave a cry of fright. In a panic Tom went after her but could not find her.

"Elspeth! Where are you?" he cried.

"Down here, Tom!" She had stumbled off the road and rolled down a bank on to a piece of lower-lying marshy land. Tom gave her a hand up on to the road again. Her shoes and stockings were covered in mud.

"You'd better hold on to me, Elspeth, in case either of us slips into a ditch again."

Elspeth clutched at his arm. It seemed they were not at

the cross-roads after all, but at a place where the road widened. They wandered along, listening for the sound of their feet to make sure they were still on the road, feeling for the firm foothold. They were never quite sure on which side of the road they were. At last they reached the place where the four hill-roads met. Here they usually took the road to the left which brought them to the bridge across the river. Not far away was the farm road to Birkhope. For a moment they stood uncertainly, then Tom said, "Here's the road to the left. We'll soon be at Birkhope now, Elspeth."

They trudged along for about a quarter of a mile, the mist pressing against their eyes. The road took a bend to the left. Tom stopped for a moment, bewildered. "I don't remember that bend in the road. Surely we should have come to the bridge by now?"

"I can hear water running nearby," Elspeth said.

"Then we must be near the river," Tom said with some relief. He looked on the river as a pointer by which they could find their way to the farm.

All at once they plunged off the road and Tom slipped and fell, dragging Elspeth with him. They were in a sedgy meadow with tussocks of tawny grass rising about them. Tom struggled to his feet and gave a gasp of pain.

"What's the matter?" Elspeth cried.

"I've—I've twisted my ankle." It was only with great pain that Tom could take a step, but he knew they *must* get back to the road. The fog swirled and eddied about them, ever thicker. At last, with a hand on Elspeth's shoulder, he managed to take a few halting steps.

"We must be quite near the road," Elspeth said encouragingly, but even the next few steps did not bring them back on the road again. They both realized the horrid truth at the same time.

"Tom! We've lost the road now. I don't know which way to turn."

"I think we must be heading away from it," Tom decided.

They turned and stumbled in the opposite direction but still they did not come to the road. The sound of water came nearer and nearer. The ground began to slope steeply beneath their feet. Of a sudden Tom clutched at Elspeth, holding her back.

"Wait, Elspeth! Don't move!"

For a second a gap was torn in the swirling mist. There, below them, the river rushed and eddied about its jagged rocks, deep and dark!

"Oh, Tom! Another few steps and we'd have been in the water!" Elspeth covered her eyes with her hands.

"It was lucky we stopped when we did," Tom said soberly.

They backed away from the water a step or two at a time, climbing the bank till they reached the sedge-grown meadow again. Over the tufts of coarse grass they stumbled, holding on to each other, afraid where yet another false step might plunge them. Sometimes the sound of the river seemed nearer, sometimes further away. At last they seemed to be going uphill and the ground felt harder.

"Maybe we're coming to the road at last," Elspeth said breathlessly, but there was no sign of the road. Instead they almost fell into some broom bushes.

"I—I can't go on, Elspeth. My ankle hurts a lot," Tom had to admit. "This ground seems pretty dry and the grass is short. Let's rest a bit and try shouting to get help."

They sat down by the bushes and began to cry "Help! Help! Come and find us! Help!"

At Birkhope Mrs. Meggetson had watched the mist close round the farm-steading. With anxious eyes she peered through the kitchen window as it thickened and blotted out the landscape. Now and again she cast a glance at the clock. When the time came and passed for Tom and Elspeth to return, she went to the door and tried to penetrate the white wool of the fog.

"John! John!" she cried.

John Meggetson came from the byre where he had been milking the cows.

"What's wrong, lass?"

"The fog, John! It's thicker than ever. The bairns have not come back. It's an hour past their time and there's no sign of them."

John Meggetson looked slightly uneasy but he tried to laugh off his wife's fears.

"Maybe they're just playing in the school yard. You know what bairns are! Perhaps they've been kept in for careless work."

"On a night like this? Surely not? Mr. Donaldson always lets the children away early in bad weather."

"We can soon find out about that." Meggetson strode briskly to the telephone. He dialled the school-house number and Mr. Donaldson replied.

"Were the children away from the school at the usual time, Mr. Donaldson? Tom and Elspeth haven't shown up yet and the wife's getting a bit anxious as the fog's thickening."

When Mr. Donaldson answered John exclaimed urgently, "What's that you're telling me? An hour *earlier* than usual? Then they should have been home nigh on two hours ago. Where can they have got?"

"What is it, John?" Mrs. Meggetson asked in a voice that was sharp with anxiety.

"Wheesht, lass! Let me hear what Mr. Donaldson says." He listened for a minute, then replied, "Right, Mr. Donaldson!

I'll do that. Aye, I'll bring a torch, for dark's beginning
to fall. You'll go as far as the cross-roads too? Right! I'll
meet you there." He put down the receiver and turned to
his wife. "The children left school an hour earlier because
of the fog. I'm going to look for them, lass. Mr. Donaldson
is going to search along the road from his end too. I'll take
Jeff wi' me." He took his stick and made for the door.
Suddenly Flash was whimpering at his heels.

"Take Flash with you!" his wife said. "If anyone can
find Tom it will be Flash."

Flash gave an eager whine as if he understood.

"I'll take them both. Flash can go on the lead and Jeff
can trot behind. Cheer up, wumman! There's no cause to
look doleful. They'll just have strayed off the path."

"The river was in spate today," Jane Meggetson reminded
him. "Pray God they haven't gone down by the river!"

"Come on, Flash! We'll fetch Tom." Meggetson snapped
on the lead. Flash barked eagerly and as soon as they were
outside, he tugged at the lead, setting a pace that John
Meggetson found hard to follow in the fog.

"Steady, Flash, lad! Take it easy!"

When they reached the main road Flash turned without
hesitation in the direction of the school until he reached
the cross-roads. There he stopped abruptly and cast around,
sniffing at the road. Meggetson gave him the length of the
lead and held Jeff in check. All at once Flash plunged along
one of the roads.

"No, Flash, that's not the road they'd take," Uncle
John told him. "That road leads away from the farm,
alongside the river."

Flash only tugged the harder, barked and whined and
turned and snapped at the restraining lead.

"You want off the lead, Flash? Ye're a sensible dog and

you'll have a reason. I'll slip the lead on Jeff instead and we'll follow ye." Holding Flash by the collar, Meggetson transferred the lead to Jeff, then he let Flash go. Nose pointing to the ground, Flash set off along the side road.

Tom and Elspeth huddled beside the bushes, wet and cold, shouting in turn, "Help! We're down here! Help!" Tom's ankle was painful and beginning to swell.

"We can't make anybody hear us. There might be no one for miles. I'll have to try crawling, Elspeth."

"We just don't know which way to crawl, Tom—" Elspeth began and then she broke off abruptly, "Listen!"

From the distance there came a bark.

"It's Flash!" Tom cried. "I'd know Flash's bark anywhere. Flash! Flash!" he yelled at the top of his voice.

There was an answering crescendo of barks coming nearer. Then, out of the mist, Flash burst upon them, springing upon Tom, licking his face, barking for joy, jumping upon Elspeth with delight.

"Oh, Flash! Flash!" Tom hugged him close. The tears of relief chased each other down Elspeth's cheeks.

"I wonder if he came from the farm all by himself?" Tom said.

Flash barked again and whined, running a few steps away from them, then turning back as though he wanted them to follow him. Then, at a distance from out the fog came an answering bark.

"That's Jeff!" Tom exclaimed. "Uncle John can't be far away. Shout, Elspeth, shout! Make Jeff hear us!"

Together they shouted "Jeff!" and "Uncle John!" and Flash added a torrent of excited barking. Out of the mist loomed Uncle John, piloted by Jeff on the lead and with him, wonder of wonders, was Mr. Donaldson.

"Just as Flash disappeared into the mist Mr. Donaldson caught up with me at the cross-roads," Uncle John told them. "But it was Flash found ye. It was wonderful the way he knew you'd turned up the wrong road. I never dreamed you'd go that way."

"We nearly fell into the river," Tom said soberly.

"Tom's sprained his ankle. That's why we couldn't move from here," Elspeth told them. Mr. Donaldson examined it.

"Yes, it's swollen. I think if your uncle and I link hands we can make a kind of chair for you, Tom, if you hang on to us. At least we can get you back to the road, though it's a fair step from there back to Birkhope."

"That's all right. Once we get him to the road, if you'll wait wi' him, Mr. Donaldson, I'll away up to the farm and bring down the horse to carry him."

"Yes, I'll do that. But will you find your way all right?"

"Oh, aye! I ken these roads like the palm o' my hand and Jeff'll guide us on the lead. Ye're shivering, Elspeth, my lass! Ye'd better come along wi' me and let the missus get you into some warm dry clothes."

It was a tired but happy party that sat round the fire at Birkhope that night, the children in thick dressing gowns, drinking hot milk and Uncle John eating his belated supper. Stretched out on the hearthrug were Jeff and Flash. Flash lay close to Tom's bandaged ankle.

"Good dog, Flash!" Tom said.

"Do you think both dogs might have a chocolate drop, Mr. Meggetson," Elspeth asked coaxingly.

"Weel now, I think they might," Mr. Meggetson agreed, "But mind, now, ye're no' to make a habit o' it." He solemnly winked one eye at Aunt Jane. Flash thumped his white-tipped tail on the floor for sheer happiness.

6

UNDER AUNT JANE'S treatment Tom's sprained ankle soon recovered, though it was a week before he could walk as far as the school, but Mr. Donaldson sent him lessons by Elspeth.

The tawny bracken on the hillsides faded to a drab grey-brown and the white rime appeared on the grass as the children made their way to school. The weeks sped by and still Elspeth was with them. Mrs. Young had been sent to a convalescent hospital after her treatment in the general hospital was finished. Aunt Jane had got so used to having Elspeth about the house that she declared it was like having another daughter and she would miss her terribly when she had to go home again.

All that autumn Flash's training continued. Every week-end Tom and his uncle took him out among the sheep on the hills. He learned to gather a flock and bring them in a compact bunch down the hill; to herd them between gates and to pen them.

"What I like about Flash is that he doesna' *fuss*," Uncle John remarked. "Some dogs get the sheep all flustered and leaping about, but no' Flash."

"Do you think he'll be good enough for the Sheep Dog Trials next year, Uncle John?" Tom asked anxiously.

"For the local Trials? Mebbe! Mebbe! We'll see how he shapes first. He's got a lot to learn yet."

"He can drive the sheep into a pen jolly well *now*." Tom was a trifle nettled.

"Aye, but that's not all. He's got to learn singling next."

"What's that?"

"To separate a sheep from the flock and bring it out. Ye've seen Jeff do it."

"Just *any* sheep?"

"The sheep that's wanted. The one I point out to him. Look, Tom, we'll give Flash a turn in the paddock again this afternoon with just five sheep and show him how to bring one of them to us. That's the most difficult thing he has to learn. Go ask your aunt for a red ribbon."

Tom was mystified. "Why do you want a red ribbon?"

"To mark the sheep that's to be singled out from the others. That's how they mark a sheep in the Trials, so Flash had better get used to it."

"But you don't go round marking sheep with red ribbons when you want them bringing out of the flock," Tom objected.

"No! You point the stick at that particular sheep. The pointed stick is enough to show the dog which one. But at the Trials the *judges* need the red ribbon to make sure that the dog has brought the right one. They're not so clever as the dog!" Uncle John chuckled.

"I've got a red ribbon," Elspeth said, taking one from her own hair.

"Thanks, Elspeth. Are you coming to watch?"

"I'd love to," Elspeth said eagerly.

"We'll take Jeff. If Flash watches him, he'll soon learn what's needed. Come along! Let's get cracking!" Uncle John said.

They went to the paddock where Meggetson kept the five sheep ready for Flash's training. They were not always the same five sheep, partly because sheep can get used to commands as well as a dog, and partly for another reason.

"Flash'll have to learn to handle other people's sheep at the Trials, so the more changes we can give him, the better," Uncle John decided. "Some sheep obey more quickly than others. He'll have to get used to all kinds."

Flash, on the lead, watched Jeff running free and gathering the sheep. He gave a "Wuff!" to remind Tom and Uncle John that he was waiting and willing.

"It's all right, Flash. Your turn will come," Uncle John promised him.

Once the sheep were penned in a corner of the field Uncle John fastened the red ribbon round the neck of one and then drew back, taking Jeff behind him. Then he pointed with his stick and said "Fetch him, Jeff!"

Jeff looked at the pointing stick and the sheep and went after him into the corner. He fixed his eye on the sheep which retreated before him. As Jeff advanced, the be-ribboned sheep separated from the other sheep. Jeff cornered him neatly and gave a look at his master as though waiting for instruction.

"That's right, Jeff. Fetch him to me!" Uncle John pointed at the sheep again, then waved the stick towards himself.

Jeff neatly headed the sheep round towards him, driving back the other four sheep by his threatening attitude when-ever they tried to break out into the field too. The be-ribboned sheep trotted out obediently towards Uncle John, who took a hold of it by the scruff of the neck and said "Good dog, Jeff!" Jeff sat down, thumping his tail and well pleased by the word of praise.

Uncle John repeated the performance twice for Flash's benefit. By the third time Jeff brought the sheep out with a slightly bored air. Flash, on the other hand, was becoming more and more restive. He strained on his lead towards the sheep.

"Right, now, Tom! Flash has seen what Jeff did. You try him now. Point with the stick to the sheep and tell him to fetch the sheep to you. Wait a minute, though. Let Jeff bunch the sheep first."

When the sheep were grouped, with the one wearing the red ribbon on the far side, Tom pointed with the stick and said, "Fetch him, Flash! Fetch him to me!" Then he slipped the lead off Flash. For a moment Flash looked doubtfully from Tom to the sheep and Tom repeated his commands, emphasizing them by jabbing with his stick in the direction of the sheep. Then the idea clicked in Flash's mind that *Tom* wanted the sheep. Jeff had brought it out for Uncle John. Now *he* was to bring it out for Tom. He gave a quick glance from the stick to the sheep, then he was in among the little flock. He pranced about in front of the marked sheep until he had him separated from the rest. With a sharp "Wuff!" he turned the sheep away from the others and down the hill to Tom.

"Aye, aye, no' bad! No' bad at all for a first try!" Uncle John commented. "But he'll have to learn how to do it more quietly, not so much leaping about and he'll not have to bark, either."

"But isn't it natural for a dog to bark?" Elspeth asked.

"Aye, mebbe, but at the Trials the judges would take marks off for a dog that fussed and barked, so it's better to train the dog not to bark at all. Barking upsets the sheep."

"How can I train him not to bark?" Tom asked, almost in despair.

"Reprove him by saying 'No! No!' when he does bark, and only praise him when he doesn't. If the worst came to it, you could put a muzzle on him when he's learning singling, but that often annoys a dog. See if ye can train him first by showing you are *not* pleased when he barks. You could even pretend to be angry and to shake the stick. Mind, though, *never* strike him wi' it."

"Of course Tom wouldn't!" Elspeth said indignantly, then coloured at daring to speak like that to Mr. Meggetson.

Uncle John smiled. "No, I don't think he would, Elspeth. The thing is that Flash takes his *directions* from that stick, which way it points and moves. If he learns that when it's shaken Tom is not pleased, then Flash will try to do better. He's an intelligent dog." He turned to Tom. "Weel, Tom, shall we let Flash have another go at it?"

This time Flash got the sheep cornered with less difficulty and actually crouched on the ground before him, fixing the sheep with his eye.

"That's fine! That's fine! He's got the sheep under control with his eye. The power of the eye, Tom! Now tell him to fetch the sheep to you."

Flash barked again but not so lustily as before. Tom at once cried in ringing tones, "No, no, Flash! Quiet!" and shook the stick vigorously. At first the dog was puzzled and was at a loss to know what was wrong, then, when almost by a miracle, he brought the sheep in with a subdued growl, Tom knew the lesson was almost learned.

"That's the way, Tom. He's had enough for now, but stick at it. Give him a lesson each day till he can single out the sheep without fuss or noise."

"What about——" Elspeth began.

Uncle John anticipated what she was going to say and shook his head. "No, my lassie! No chocolate drop for

Flash today! You must wait till he's learned his lesson properly. When Tom praises him, then you can reward him."

Elspeth pouted a little but Tom said quietly, "Uncle John's right, you know. Flash has to learn."

The year wore on to Christmas and the school holidays. There had been one or two flurries of snow but nothing more than a sugar-dusting of the ground. With the beginning of the holidays, however, the skies took on a steely grey colour and the wind was bitter cold. Mrs. Meggetson sniffed the air and shivered as she crossed the farm-yard with Tom and Elspeth after feeding the hens.

"There's snow in that wind, John!" she cried to her husband as he came from the byre.

"Aye, lass! I'm no' liking the look of it at all."

"Och! It may only be a shower," she said. "It'll be warmer once the snow is out."

"There'll be more than a slight fall, I fear." He cast a glance at the surrounding hills. "Look! The sheep are beginning to move down from the high land of their own accord."

"Guid sakes! So they are!" Mrs. Meggetson exclaimed.

"Why? What does that mean?" Tom asked.

"Sheep can tell when there's a bad storm coming and they start making for the lower ground to find shelter. They're no' daft, are sheep! I'll need to get Andra and round up the flocks and bring them down."

Andra was the shepherd.

"Do you think it's going to be as bad as that?" Aunt Jane asked.

"It could be! If there's snow, there'll be bad drifting with that wind. The sheep'll be better in the fields round the farm steading. It's easier to take food to them than to haul it up the hill, and we'll have to handfeed them if the grass is covered by snow."

"Uncle John, can I come with you too?" Tom asked.

Meggetson hesitated a moment. Tom could not go as fast as he and Andra. It called for hardihood and endurance too in the teeth of that bitter gale. On the other hand Flash was proving himself a useful dog and an extra hand with a dog might be a good help.

"All right, Tom," he agreed, "but if you canna' make the pace, you're to tell me and come back to the farm."

"Put on your warmest sweater and coat, Tom, and take a sack to cover your head and shoulders if the snow comes down," Aunt Jane advised him.

Uncle John, with Tom and the two dogs, strode uphill to find Andra, the shepherd. Tom found his breathing cut him like a knife as he tried to keep up with his uncle. The keen wind stung his face till it smarted and his hands became numb with the cold. Not for the world, though, would Tom have turned back! Only the dogs, unrestrained by the lead, seemed to enjoy it as they ran free side by side.

Before they reached the summit of the nearest hill the flakes of snow began to fall. At first it was a thin wetting sleet that seemed to penetrate to the very bones, then the flakes began to fall thicker. Tom was glad of the sack to protect his head and shoulders. Every now and again he could remove it and shake off the burden of snow. They moved up to the crest of the hill to get close in to the sheep to drive them down.

"Awa' there!" Uncle John shouted and off went Jeff in a wide cast to come in behind the sheep.

"Send Flash off to your left!" Uncle John yelled to Tom above the keening of the wind.

"Come by, Flash! Come by!" Tom shouted waving his stick.

The two dogs met behind the flock and began to run to

and fro behind the sheep, working them steadily downhill.
Jeff had already accepted Flash as a partner in this task.

When they had got the first flock about half-way down
towards the farm Uncle John asked, "Do you think you and
Flash could take this lot down to the steading and pen them
in the paddock, Tom? That would leave Andra and me to
fetch in the far-away flocks on Kiplaw. Can ye manage it?"

"I think I can with Flash to help."

"Make sure he rounds up any stragglers, Tom, or we'll
be hunting for them in the snow drifts tomorrow."

"Shall we come back to you on Kiplaw afterwards?"
Tom asked.

His uncle looked at him keenly. "You've a good heart,
lad. If your strength will stand up to it, I'll be glad of your
help."

Cold as he was outside, it gave Tom a sudden warm
feeling to his heart that his uncle should need him and speak
a word of praise. He knew that John Meggetson never gave
praise unless it was earned.

"So long, then!" he said lightly. "I'll be back!" He
whistled to Flash to bring down the sheep.

The whirling snow almost blotted out the hillside before
he reached the farm but Flash's unerring instinct brought
them almost straight down to the farm road. Tom ran
ahead to open the gate into the paddock, but Elspeth was
there before him, her small tip-tilted nose a bright pink in
the bitter wind.

"I'll help you, Tom! You stay with Flash and direct
him."

Between them they got the sheep safely penned in the
paddock.

Aunt Jane appeared at the farm-house door. "Come you
in, Tom! I've got some hot broth for you."

"Sheep's heid broth?" Tom asked, giving her a grin. He had never forgotten his first meal at Birkhope.

"No, lad, it's Scotch broth this time. You'd be as weel to have a bowl too, Elspeth. You look fair nipped, lassie!"

Tom was glad of the almost scalding hot broth. It put warmth and new life into him, but as soon as he had finished the bowl, he stood up and called Flash.

"Where are you going, Tom?" Aunt Jane asked in surprise.

"Back to Uncle John!"

"Surely no'?" Aunt Jane asked in surprise. "It's a cruel hard job on yon hillside for a bit laddie. You've done your share today."

"Uncle John said he could do with my help so I'm going back," Tom said obstinately.

"Weel, if you're set on it——. Wait for a couple of minutes, though, while I fill two Thermos flasks wi' the soup. Your uncle and Andra'll be glad o' something to warm them up. Elspeth, cut a round or two of bread and cheese and put it in the shopping bag while I fill the flasks. They'll be easier carried that way. You'll manage it, Tom?"

"Sure thing!" Tom said with assumed lightness. It was a thought indeed to leave the warmth and comfort of the kitchen for the cutting cold outside. He called Flash and they went out into a world already white with snow, a world in which the familiar landmarks were fast disappearing. The snow was heavy and the leaden skies gave threat of more to come.

It was a gruelling job mounting the steep slopes of Kiplaw, carrying the bag and at the same time holding on to Flash's lead. Flash tugged upward all the time. Tom did not let him off the lead, for he knew Flash would guide him to Jeff and his uncle, even though the hillside was a whirling white cloud. Tom was almost spent when Flash gave an eager "Wuff!" and there was an answering bark from Jeff. Then John Meggetson's figure emerged from the snowy cloud.

"You there, Tom? Did you make it, lad, after all?" There was a note of pleased surprise in his voice.

"Aye, Uncle John. I've brought you some broth in these flasks, and some cheese and bread."

"That's right welcome!" John Meggetson took the flask from him. "We're having a bit o' difficulty wi' the sheep, Tom. Some of them have gone down into Blythe's Gully and it's a job winkling them all out. I've got a part o' the flock here and Jeff's holding them while Andra has gone after the rest wi' his dog. If you could do another journey down wi' the sheep here, then I could join Andra hunting up the other part o' the flock."

"Can't I go down into Blythe's Gully?" Tom asked.

Uncle John shook his head doubtfully. "It needs someone who knows the ground, Tom. The snow's beginning to drift there already. You'd be of more use to me if ye'd take these sheep down. Put them in the long pasture behind the house."

Blythe's Gully was a steepsided valley that ran beside a stream, a long bracken-filled hollow like a deep furrow on the hillside. Though Tom would have liked to hunt up the missing sheep, he saw the sense of his uncle's decision.

"All right, Uncle John!" He loosed Flash from the lead. "Come away to me, Flash!" In an instant Flash vanished into the snow as he cast round the flock to bring them downhill. The flock moved steadily downward, marshalled by Tom and Flash. For a moment Uncle John stood watching them as they disappeared into the snowy haze.

The flock could not be hurried as Flash had to keep an

eye on the fringes of it to make sure no sheep strayed. Flash ran to and fro behind them, giving an occasional low growl at any sheep that seemed to be splitting off from the main herd. The tireless little dog kept the flock in a neat compact bunch with only a shout of direction now and again from Tom. Tom's whole body ached unbearably in the bitter cold wind and his legs felt as though they would give way under him as he plodded through the deepening snow. He was so tired that he almost wept with relief when the chimneys of Birkhope came within sight.

Elspeth was faithfully watching for him through the window. As soon as she saw the grey mass of the approaching flock coming down the last slope of the hill, she flung on her coat, seized a stick and rushed out to assist Tom.

"Hullo, Elspeth!" Tom greeted her wearily. "We're to put this lot in the long pasture behind the house, Uncle John says."

With her stick Elspeth helped to guide the herd along the narrow farm lane. She opened the gate and Flash redoubled his efforts on the flanks of the herd till the last leaping obstinate sheep was safely through. When at last the gate was finally shut on them, it was all Tom could do to hobble to the farmhouse.

Aunt Jane saw he was all in. "Get into that chair, Tom," she directed, pulling round the armchair to the fire. "I'll bring tea to you."

"Let me take off your boots," Elspeth said and she knelt at his feet and took off his rubber boots and sodden stockings. She brought a towel and rubbed briskly at his numbed feet till life and warmth began to ebb back into them again.

Aunt Jane produced a huge cup of very sweet tea. "Take that, Tom. There's plenty of sugar in it to revive you." Tom drank it gratefully.

"Would you like to go to bed?" his aunt asked.

"Not till Uncle John gets back."

Aunt Jane cast an anxious glance at the leaden dusk creeping early round the windows. "He may be a while yet. I'll go and fetch a change of dry clothes for you and you can strip by the fire instead of in the cold bedroom. You'll have the kitchen to yourself. I'm going with Elspeth to feed the hens and shut them in the hen-house before the snow gets any thicker. Just leave your clothes on the hearthrug. I'll collect them and put them up to dry."

The door shut behind them both. It was a relief to get into warm dry clothes but by the time it was done, Tom was glad to sink back into the chair again. He was almost asleep when his aunt and Elspeth came back. He struggled back to consciousness to ask, "You'll see Flash gets his supper, Elspeth?"

"Don't worry, Tom. I'm warming up a meat stew for him now," Elspeth told him.

Elspeth set the bowl down beside Flash who took it hungrily, then wagged his tail in gratitude. Elspeth dived into her pocket.

"Do you think Flash could have a chocolate drop, Tom?"

"Yes, he's deserved it," Tom said sleepily. He opened his eyes to see Flash take the chocolate, then lick Elspeth's hand gratefully. Tom gave Elspeth a warm smile, then almost at once he was fast asleep with Flash stretched out at his feet, fast asleep too.

The dark had fallen before John Meggetson arrived home. He had brought another twenty sheep to the steading. When he opened the door Aunt Jane gave a sigh of relief.

"At last ye're hame, John!"

"Aye, lass! It's getting thicker on the hills. Tom's back

all right? I see he got the sheep penned in the long pasture."

Aunt Jane pointed to Tom, fast asleep in the big armchair.

"He was fair beat, poor lad! I wonder he didn't drop in his tracks. John, why did you let him do so much? He's only a laddie."

"There was no holding him back," John Meggetson said as he took off his leggings. "Tom and Flash did a grand job. If it hadna' been for them, I doubt if we could have brought so many sheep down from the hills."

"Did ye get them all?" Aunt Jane enquired sharply.

"No, lass! There are some of them in Blythe's Gully where it branches into Fox Nick and it's right steep there. Wi' the weather thickening we had to bring down the sheep we'd gathered."

"How many do you think are missing?"

Meggetson considered a minute. "I reckon there'll be about thirty of them."

Aunt Jane looked serious. Thirty sheep were a lot to lose.

"Will you get them out of the gully, do you think?"

"I don't know. The weather's worsening. The snow's falling faster and there's a gale blowing too."

"Aye, and that means drifting," his wife remarked.

That night the wind whined and shrieked round the rooftops of the old farm and the snow fell silently, relentlessly. When Tom woke next morning he peered through his window on a white and unrecognizable world. The wind had blown the snow into drifts against the byre and sheep pens. Early though it was, John Meggetson was astir. Tom saw his uncle cross the farm-yard to the barn. Tom flung on his clothes and ran down to the kitchen. Aunt Jane was trying to chivvy some life into the fire which she had banked up with coal dust and peat the previous night so that it smouldered into a blossoming red. Well she knew the fire would be needed to dry clothes and perhaps to revive some half-dead sheep.

"What's Uncle John doing?" Tom asked as he pulled on his boots. "Is he going after the lost sheep?"

"Not yet. He's going to feed the sheep pastured round the steading first. The poor things canna' get at the grass for the snow."

"What'll they eat, then?"

"Why, neeps, lad, swedes and kale! He's cutting up the neeps now."

"I'll go and help him," Tom said. He found his uncle in an outhouse chopping turnips in half.

"Hullo, Tom!"

"I've come to lend you a hand, uncle."

"Thanks, lad. We'll have to get food to the ewes—the lambs will be born poor skinny creatures if their mothers havena' had enough to eat."

Tom eyed the heap of turnips on the floor. "How will you get these even to the nearby fields, Uncle John? The snow's already more than a foot deep. You couldn't push a barrow through it."

"We'll have to haul the neeps on yon sledge, Tom." His uncle pointed to a large wooden sledge in the corner.

Just then Elspeth joined them. "Can I be doing something to help, Mr. Meggetson?"

Uncle John eyed her hands. "You've got your gloves on? Good! Handling neeps is right cold work. Pile up the cut neeps on the sledge, there's a good lass."

While they cut the turnips Elspeth stacked them on the sledge.

"That's enough," John Meggetson said when the turnips began to roll off the sledge. "Now I'll haul it along to the pasture and you two can help to scatter the neeps in long rows on top of the snow."

As he slowly hauled the sledge over the snow Tom and Elspeth took up armfuls of the cut turnips and scattered them beside the sheep. Before long the sheep were eating them hungrily.

"Fine! Fine! They'll come to no harm now. That's a good job done," Uncle John declared, when they had made several journeys with the sledge. "There's your aunt at the kitchen door crying on us to come for our breakfast. You should have grand appetites for it the day!"

Never had oatmeal porridge and fried ham and eggs tasted so good to Tom! As soon as Uncle John had finished, however, he did not take time to smoke his usual pipe of tobacco but rose from his chair.

"I'm awa' to try and locate those missing ewes now," he told his wife.

"Where do you think they'll be, Uncle John?" Tom asked.

"Dear knows, lad! There are several small gullies on the higher ground where the land drains to Blythe's Gully. This drifting snow will have filled them and the sheep could be in any of them, covered by the snow."

"But won't they suffocate?" Tom exclaimed.

"No, they could stay alive in a drift for days, provided they don't try to climb out over each other's back and break their hearts with exhaustion. There was once a flock of sheep found in a drift standing on each other's backs, three or four deep, all dead wi' struggling. Ah, weel, I'll awa' and meet Andra at the top o' the hill. Let's hope we can *see* where the gully is."

"Won't you be able to do that?" Tom asked surprised.

"It may have been filled in level with the rest o' the

hillside and the first way we might find it is by falling into a deep drift."

"I'd like to come too," Tom said.

"Weel, if ye stay close by me and take a shepherd's crook with you, maybe you'd get along."

"What's the shepherd's crook for?"

"If ye're doubtful of what lies before you—and ye could easily step into a deep drift in the gully,—you probe wi' the crook in front o' ye. If you canna' touch the ground wi' it, turn back right quickly. It's as simple as that."

They each took a crook and Uncle John shouldered a spade too and then set off up the hillside, Flash and Jeff following at their heels.

"You follow in my footsteps, Tom, like the chap in the Christmas carol followed after good King Wenceslas," Uncle John advised. "I don't say your feet will be any warmer but if I drop into a drift ye'll see me in time to step back."

John Meggetson seemed to have an uncanny knowledge of the hillside paths even under the snow, but it was tough going all the same. They sank up to the ankles at every step.

A dog barked near the top of the hill and there was Andra, the shepherd, coming to meet them with his dog, Don.

"They might be down there, Mr. Meggetson," Andra said, pointing with his crook to what seemed a smooth layer of snow. Uncle John advanced cautiously holding his crook in front of him and probing into the snow drift at every step. All at once the crook sank over a yard into the snow!

"Aye, there's a gully, Andra, right enough! Watch your step behind me, Tom! I'll try moving along where the edge of the gully ought to be."

Suddenly Uncle John sank up to his waist in the soft snow!

Tom gave a cry of dismay but in a moment Andra was beside him.

"Steady, lad!" Andra held out the crook of his staff to Uncle John who also held out his crook to Andra. Andra hauled on both of them till, like a cork out of a bottle, Uncle John came out of the drift.

"Are you hurt, Uncle John?"

"Mercy me, no, lad! It was like falling into a feather bed, only I'm glad I didna' disappear altogether. Wait, though, Andra! I thought I felt something stirring under my foot. I'm going to probe my way forward again."

"Catch the hold o' my crook, then, Mr. Meggetson," Andra suggested.

Holding with one hand to Andra's crook and probing ahead with his own a foot at a time, John Meggetson moved forward. Suddenly he gave an excited cry. "See that!"

The crook that was in his hand seemed to have shot upward about nine inches of its own accord!

"There's a sheep under there!" Uncle John declared.

Jeff evidently thought so too, for he jumped down into the snow and began digging and scratching with his feet. Don joined him, and Flash, after an enquiring yelp, joined the pair of them in the shallow hole. The three dogs scattered the snow in all directions.

"Aye, the dogs know right enough! I'm going in again, Andra. If a sheep can stand there, so can I!"

Uncle John let himself cautiously down into the hollow beside the dogs. Though he sank up to his knees in the drift he did not go any further.

"Hand me the spade, Andra," he said.

He dug away vigorously, flinging the snow as far from

him as he could. Suddenly there was a stir in the snow itself as though a small earthquake was going on, and out came the astonished head and shoulders of a black-faced ewe! A few more spadefuls of snow and the animal was liberated and went bounding away on to higher ground!

"Let Flash go after her and hold her, Tom. We don't want her disappearing into another drift," Uncle John directed.

Tom called, "Away to me, Flash! Fetch the sheep!" and pointed at the ewe floundering in the snow. In a moment Flash had bounded after her and turned her. He crouched down before her, holding her with the menacing power of his eye.

Jeff went on scratching furiously in the hole, making the snow fly.

"More than one, eh, Jeff?" Uncle John said. He advanced a cautious couple of steps with the spade and dug about again. Out came another ewe, then a third and a fourth till ten of them were beside Tom. Flash concentrated on keeping them in a compact group, giving a low growl at any sheep that seemed inclined to frisk away.

"That's the lot there, I think. I'm striking what seems like rock with the spade. Well, that's ten saved anyway," Uncle John said as he climbed out of the hole and dusted the powdered snow from his clothes. "We'll move down the hill a bit to where the Lynn Cleuch joins the Blythe Gully."

With the three dogs moving the retrieved flock they descended the hill for about a quarter of a mile, then, at a place that looked to Tom to be just a continuation of the wide expanse of snow, Uncle John stopped.

"The Lynn Cleuch should be just about here. We'll feel about for it with our crooks, Andra."

"Is it very deep?" Tom asked.

"No, lad. It's just a shallow wee burn where a trickle o' water runs, three feet deep, no more, but that's enough to shelter and hide sheep if they get under the lee of its bank."

Carefully the shepherd and Uncle John felt about with their crooks, but found no hollow that might be the Cleuch.

Tom had put Flash on a lead so that he did not interfere with the other two dogs who had the little flock under their control. All at once Flash began to whine and strain at the lead.

"What's wrong with you, Flash? Come behind!" Tom ordered him.

Flash obeyed for a couple of minutes, then the whining and straining began again. Uncle John eyed the dog curiously.

"What ails the dog? Let him off the lead, Tom."

Tom let Flash go free and immediately Flash became very excited and bounded away a dozen yards to the extreme right and began scraping and scratching furiously at the snow. Tom was about to whistle the dog back when Uncle John put a restraining hand on his arm. "Wait, lad! Let's see what he's up to. There are two or three of the sheep we used for Flash's training that are among the missing flock."

Flash was fast disappearing into the hole he was digging.

"We'll give you a bit o' help, Flash," Uncle John said and advanced with his spade. Soon he was almost waist deep digging the snow from about his feet. Flash burrowed and dug too, only pausing now and again to sniff with his nose at the hole they were making and to give an impatient little whine.

"Aye, we're getting near something," Uncle John said and began to scrape the snow away with the spade rather than to dig it, for fear of hurting any animal that might be underneath. All at once the snow drift began to move of its own accord! Out came one ewe after another till *fifteen* of them had emerged!

"Weel done, Flash! Weel done, lad!" Uncle John praised the small dog. Tom patted him with pride and added his praises to Uncle John's. Flash rolled over in the snow with delight in the praise and in his own achievement.

"I thought the dog was smelling out the sheep he knew so weel," Uncle John remarked.

"Could he really tell them from the other sheep by their smell?" Tom asked.

"Aye, lad. I reckon Jeff can tell every single sheep in my flock by its own scent. This proves Flash is going to be equally good. He knew his particular sheep too. Aye, he's got the makings of a grand sheep dog. Weel, there are still five sheep unaccounted for, and one of them's the ram. We'll hunt round for a while longer with Flash, while Jeff and Don keep the sheep we've found."

Though they cast about over the snowy hillside and followed the watercourse down the hill as best they could for the drifted snow banks, Meggetson probing continually, they did not find any more sheep. Flash seemed to have lost interest in Lynn Cleuch too. Already the early dusk seemed to be drawing around them.

"We can do no more today," Uncle John decided. "After all, it's no' bad to have found twenty-five out o' thirty missing sheep in weather like this. There'll be many more sheep lost on the Border hills this day. We can count ourselves lucky. I wish we hadna' lost the ram, though. He was a good animal."

Tom remembered that when his uncle had met him at the Waverley Station in Edinburgh, he had just bought the ram.

They went steadily down, the two older dogs having command of the flock. Flash kept to heel behind Tom. Only once did he stop and whine and give a short sharp bark. Tom thought it was because he wished to be at work with the other dogs behind the flock. "Come on, Flash!" he said, and Flash obeyed with a certain reluctance.

They reached the farm steading and penned the sheep with the others in the large paddock. Andra shouted "goodnight" and went to his own cottage.

Aunt Jane had done them proud with Cock-a-Leekie broth and stewed chicken, Elspeth had made a boiled apple dumpling. Never had a meal tasted so good to Tom! There was a good helping of meat for the dogs too, and after it Flash and Jeff fell asleep at opposite corners of the hearthrug. After a strong cup of tea Tom began to feel drowsy too and his head to nod on his chest.

"Off to bed with you, lad! You'll fall off your chair next!" Aunt Jane told him kindly.

Tom woke up enough to bestow his usual good-night pat on Flash who looked up at him with eyes full of dog-like adoration. He gave Tom a quick loving lick.

"You know, that dog owns Tom as weel as Tom owning the dog!" Uncle John told Aunt Jane as the door shut behind Tom.

7 TOM AND FLASH BOTH HAVE HUNCHES

IT WAS JUST as the first pale light began to streak over the dark winter sky that Tom woke up suddenly and sat bolt upright in bed. He had been dreaming that he and Flash were looking for the lost ram.

"The hollow? The hollow half-way down the hill where the gorse bushes are?" Tom exclaimed. "That was where Flash gave a whine and a bark. I wonder?"

Quietly he got out of bed and dressed. He crept in stockinged feet on to the landing. Though he made no noise the stairs creaked under his tread. Uncle John, tired out after the previous day's work, never stirred, nor did Aunt Jane. Only Elspeth heard the creaking stair. She wondered if someone could be ill and rose and flung on her dressing gown and crept down the stair too.

Tom was just putting the kettle on the glowing fire which Aunt Jane stacked with peats at night. He was reaching for the tea-pot when Elspeth slipped into the room.

"Tom! What on earth are you up to?"

"I'm having a warm drink before I go to hunt for Uncle John's ram."

"Tom! He'd be wild if he thought you were going out alone in the half-dark. You know its dangerous on the hills in drifting snow."

Tom hesitated. "I have an idea where the ram might be."

"Well, can't he wait till after breakfast?"

"It was Flash gave me the notion. I—I'd like to prove he's as clever as I think he is."

"Och! You and your dog!" Elspeth said, but there was good-natured kindness in her voice. "All the same, it's no' safe for you to go among the gullies on the hills alone. Suppose you fell down one? Who would know where to look for you?"

"I'm going all the same," Tom said with steely obstinacy.

"Oh, no, you're not!" Elspeth said with equal determination.

"You can't stop me!" Tom told her with a flash of temper.

"Can I no'?" Elspeth picked up the poker. "I only need to clatter this among the fire-irons and shout at the top o' my voice, and that would soon bring your uncle out o' his bed!"

Tom resorted to coaxing. "Don't do that, Elspeth. Uncle John's had a tough two days of it. He needs his sleep."

"All right! So do you! Back to your bed then!"

Tom stared at the small lass he had always found so gentle and who was all at once so grim and determined.

"Elspeth, you don't understand. This is a thing I feel I've *got* to do. Please, please don't stop me going. I promise I'll be careful."

Elspeth had sudden inspiration. "All right, you can go if you'll take me with you. Two'll be safer than one. At least I'll know where you are if you fall into Blythe's Gully."

"No, no, Elspeth! It's no job for a girl."

"Listen, Tom Stokes!" Elspeth and Tom conducted the argument in hissing whispers. "I was running on these hills before you knew anything about them. I've lived here all my days. Either you take me with you, or you don't go!"

"Very well!" Tom agreed at last reluctantly.

"Right! Then I'm going to put on my outdoor clothes and you can make the tea while you're waiting for me. And don't you try to go without me or I'll wake your uncle!"

A few minutes later, after drinking the tea, Tom said, "Come on, Flash!" Flash was quite ready and Jeff gave a whine to indicate he was willing too, but Tom shook his head at him and said, "Not this time, Jeff!" They set off, Elspeth closing the door quietly behind them. They took a spade and Uncle John's crook from an outhouse and the stick Tom used, and plodded through the snow of the lower meadows, sinking in it almost to their knees. Tom carried the spade and stick and Elspeth the shepherd's crook. They reached the hillside where the wind had blown the snow into drifts almost like waves, leaving parts of the ground thinly covered. By keeping to these parts they were able to move with greater speed. It was still dark, with a ghostly greyness seeping through the night.

It seemed an eternity before they reached the clump of pine trees part way up the hill. Both children were wet and cold and the muscles of their legs ached almost unbearably. Flash followed faithfully in their wake.

"Do you want to go back, Elspeth?" Tom asked, looking at her anxiously.

Elspeth shook her head with determination. "Indeed, no, Tom Stokes!" Just then Tom plunged well past his waist into a drift!

"Oh, Tom!" Elspeth cried in a panic.

"It's all right, Elspeth. Don't come too close or you'll fall in too! Take the spade and dig towards me." Tom flung the spade to her.

Elspeth dug feverishly and found that Tom had stumbled down a steep bank. Flash dug too, around Tom, scattering the snow with his feet. Tom scraped the snow away from about him with his hands. Luckily the snow had not hardened into ice but it took several minutes of anxious digging to make a path towards Tom and to loosen the snow about his legs.

"Give me the end of the crook now. I think I can work myself free if you pull, Elspeth."

Elspeth passed the crook to him and pulled with might and main. Tom struggled forward and then came out with such suddenness that he fell on his face and Elspeth sat down abruptly in the snow. The fright over, they both laughed helplessly, partly with relief.

"All the same, Elspeth, it's a good thing you *did* come." Tom said soberly when they had done laughing. "I might have been an awfully long time getting out of the drift on my own." All at once he pointed to the hole. "Look, Elspeth, there are small stones where you have been digging. That must be the bed of the Lynn Burn. Now I know exactly where we are! It was a good thing I fell into it because it's given me my bearings now. Come on, Flash!"

Tom started off at an angle from the burn and away up the hill. After about a quarter of a mile of hard plodding Flash became excited, yelping a little and sniffing the air. He ran a few steps then came back to Tom, ran ahead again, then returned and jumped round Tom.

"This is near where he seemed a bit excited yesterday," Tom told Elspeth.

"It's as though he's wanting to lead you somewhere Tom."

They were approaching a kind of snowy hummock when Flash darted away and started scraping frantically at the snow.

"I know what it is! There's a clump of gorse bushes

there buried beneath the snow." Tom was getting excited himself. He rushed forward with the spade and started digging where Flash was scraping. Flash gave a bark as if to approve. Every time Tom paused in his digging to get breath, Flash rushed in again to scrape and scratch at the hole. Flash's scraping gave direction to Tom's digging.

"He's certainly on to something!" Tom declared.

"Give me the spade while you get a breather," Elspeth said.

They had dug quite a cave into the banked drift when Flash barked loudly. A pair of curling horns appeared in the hole!

"It's the ram!" Tom exclaimed and began to dig carefully with the spade in the animal's direction. His head emerged, and in the grey light he looked at them with an astonished baleful eye, like a sleeper newly awakened. Tom freed the snow round his legs and almost at once the ram leaped out, nearly knocking Tom over. He began to gallop away. Tom did not lose his head. "After him Flash!" he cried. "Fetch him in!"

Flash dashed round the ram, running backwards and forwards in front of him till he brought him to a halt. Then he crouched in the snow, fixing the ram with his eye.

"Hold him, Flash!" Tom ordered. He resumed the digging till he came to a gorse bush. Behind it, in a little hollow among the bushes which were covered by the drift, four ewes were cowering! Uttering wild baa-ing sounds they emerged to the light of day, only to be cornered by Flash and bunched alongside the ram!

Tom was almost delirious with delight. "The lot of them! The lot of them!" he shouted to Elspeth. "Won't Uncle John be glad? Come on! Let's get them down the hill and give him the surprise of his life."

With Flash manœuvring the sheep in a straight line down the hill, they came to their own tracks in the snow. They breasted a slight rise and there, coming up the other side of the hill towards them as fast as he could, was Uncle John with Jeff.

"What's the meaning of this?" he cried, his face very grim.

"I've got them, Uncle John! The ram and the four missing ewes!" Tom cried with pride. "They were in the hollow under the gorse bushes!"

Uncle John's face changed a little but he still shook his head at Tom. "I'm no' saying I'm not glad to see the animals and that it's a wonder you found them, but it was a right foolish thing you did, Tom! Imagine taking Elspeth off among yon terrible drifts among the hills! Your aunt was nigh off her head when I couldna' find either o' you among the farm buildings. Off into the house with you both and take Flash! I'll see these animals penned."

Tom's face fell at his uncle's reproving voice. He had felt something of a hero and now he was reduced to a foolish boy. For a moment the angry tears smarted in his eyes.

Aunt Jane came to the door and folded Elspeth in her arms.

"My lassie! My lassie! I wondered what had happened to you! Tom, you know how dangerous the hills are in deep snow. Why did you take her off like that?"

"Tom didna' take me off," Elspeth said before Tom could open his mouth to reply. "*I* told him he'd have to take me with him or I'd rouse the household."

"You're a stubborn bit lassie!" Aunt Jane scolded but her eye softened as she turned to Tom. "But why did you go, Tom?"

Tom replied rather sullenly, "I went because I thought

Flash knew where the ram was, and he was right. I knew Uncle John was worried because we hadn't found him."

John Meggetson came into the kitchen just then and he heard what Tom said. "If you knew that, why did you no' tell me last night, Tom?"

"Because it only came to me in the night and you were sleeping," Tom told him. "And—and—I thought I'd give you a pleasant surprise at breakfast time if I *could* find the ram—but it seems—it seems—you were only *vexed* about it——" Tom gulped, then rushed blindly from the room and up the stairs to his bedroom and slammed the door.

"Weel, here's a carry-on!" Uncle John exclaimed, bewildered.

"Guid sakes! Why do you have to be so thrawn wi' the laddie? He was only trying to help you," Aunt Jane told him.

"Help me? Me thrawn wi' Tom? I was right upset at what might have happened to the lad. You were little better yourself. Maybe I spoke more sharply than I meant to do."

"Och, weel, I'll just go on making the breakfast! Maybe Tom will come down when he's got his wet clothes off. Away you, Elspeth, and get into some dry things yourself."

When she was ready she tapped on Tom's door. "Are you coming down for breakfast?"

"No!"

Elspeth put her head round the door. Tom was standing staring through the window, his wet clothes unchanged.

"Och, Tom, don't be daft! Get your clothes changed, and come down."

"No!" Tom repeated fiercely.

"Why not? You'll catch your death of cold."

"Nothing I do or Flash does will ever please Uncle John.

At least he might have had a word of praise for the dog!"

"Och! Forget it! Come downstairs."

"No!" Tom replied stubbornly. "Not till I feel like it!"

"Tom, I think you're just plain stupid!" Elspeth told him and shut the door with a bang. She went down and took her place at the breakfast table.

Uncle John was eating his porridge. "Where's Tom?" he asked.

"Upstairs! He doesn't feel like coming down," Elspeth said briefly.

"Mercy me! What ails the lad?" Mrs. Meggetson exclaimed.

"If it's temper I'll go up and sort him!" Uncle John said grimly.

Elspeth laid a hand on his sleeve. "Please, Mr. Meggetson, don't be angry with Tom. He really was trying to do something to please you when he went after the ram this morning. He was trying to *help* you, truly."

"Silly young fool! He might have lost his life and yours!" Meggetson growled, but his expression became less grim.

Elspeth took courage. "I think Tom wasn't so upset by what you said as by what you *didn't* say to Flash."

"What I *didn't* say to Flash?" John Meggetson looked mystified.

"Tom said if you'd only have had a word of praise for Flash, it wouldn't have been so bad."

Uncle John looked troubled. "I'll go up and have a word wi' the laddie," he said, rising from his place.

"Now, John, go easy!" his wife warned him.

"Ye needna' worry yourself, lass!" he replied.

He tapped on Tom's bedroom door.

"What is it?" Tom's voice came truculently.

Uncle John opened the door. "I've come up to have a

word wi' ye, Tom." Tom's face flushed angrily. "Now, Tom, listen to what I have to say before you fly off the handle." Uncle John held up a restraining hand. "There's been enough trouble owing to *me* saying the first thing that came into *my* head this morning."

Tom looked up at his uncle in surprise.

"First of all, Tom, I was real glad to have those animals back, especially the ram. I think you and Flash did a good job of work. He's a grand wee dog. I'm sorry I failed to thank you for bringing them back, but ye see, lad, I was fair demented at the thought that something might have happened to *you*."

Tom turned round and looked at his uncle in astonishment. "You mean you'd been worried about *me?*"

"Aye, Tom! It mattered a lot more about you than the ram, ye know. I can get another ram any day but I canna'——" Uncle John was not given to speaking his feelings. "I've got kinda' used to having you around," he finished lamely.

"Oh, Uncle John!" Tom said warmly. He began to laugh, almost hysterically.

"Get your wet clothes off before your aunt throws a fit, and come down and have your breakfast," Uncle John directed. "I'm right keen to hear how Flash found the animals."

"I—I'll be down in a minute or two," Tom capitulated.

"Is it all right?" Aunt Jane asked anxiously when John Meggetson reappeared.

"Aye. Ye can put the lad's bacon and eggs in the pan, Uncle John replied laconically.

When the meal was ending, Uncle John asked Tom where and how the sheep were found.

"It was Flash really," Tom said modestly. "During the

night I remembered that when we were coming home, he looked towards the mound where the gorse bushes were buried and gave a little whine. I wondered about it. And he was right too!"

"Good dog!" Uncle John said, giving Flash a pat on the head. "Aye, ye'll make a grand sheep dog, right enough." He cleared his throat. "Elspeth, I've no objection to your giving Flash a chocolate drop."

Tom gave his uncle a warm, grateful look.

More snow fell before Christmas and the hills all about Birkhope stood white against a pale blue sky. Only the clumps of Douglas fir trees, which screened the farm from the northerly blasts, stood out as landmarks. The rest of the country was covered in the velvety white of the drifted snow.

"A good thing we got the sheep down from the hills when we did or we might have lost half the flock," Uncle John remarked.

They had to go on hand-feeding the sheep, for the grass was still buried. Though it was a lot of trouble to cut up turnips and kale, no one grudged the time spent on it, least of all Tom and Elspeth, who willingly lent Uncle John and Andra a hand. A new understanding seemed to have grown between Tom and his uncle.

A day or two before Christmas Aunt Jane had a quiet talk with her husband. "John, it's Christmas Day very soon. They make a lot more of Christmas in England than we do."

"Aye, we're more for celebrating the New Year."

"I—I wouldn't like Tom to feel strange here at Christmas."

"Weel, what can we do about it?" Uncle John demanded.

"I thought I'd make an extra good dinner for Christmas Day. Goose and plum-pudding like they have in England, you know."

"Michty me! What about New Year?" John Meggetson demurred.

"I don't see why we shouldn't have *two* good celebrations," Jane told him. "*You've* no cause to grumble if I cook you two good dinners. I'm all for both of them myself! And what about a present for the bairns? It's a long time since we had children in this house over Christmas."

"Heavens, wumman! What will ye think of next? Ye'll have me fair demented! How are we to get through the snow for shopping in Peebles?

"Maybe *you* could manage something without going into Peebles?"

"D'ye think my other name is Santa Claus?" Uncle John demanded. "You'll be wanting me to appear in a sledge drawn by reindeer next!"

"That's it, John! You've hit it the first time!" Aunt Jane clapped her hands. "The sledge!"

"What sledge?" John Meggetson looked mystified.

"The sledge our girls had when they were children. It's somewhere up in the loft. It probably needs a bit of repair and a coat of paint but you could manage that while the children were sleeping."

"Mm! Mm!" John pretended to think the matter over but he secretly thought it was an excellent suggestion too.

"Imagine you thinking of the sledge!" Jane Meggetson said tactfully.

John shook his head at her with a twinkle in his eye. "Jane Meggetson, ye're a crafty wumman!" All the same he went to hunt out the sledge from the pile of gear that accumulates in every farm loft.

"Mind! Don't let the bairns guess what you're doing," Aunt Jane warned him.

If John Meggetson and his wife had secrets for Christmas, so had Tom and Elspeth. Elspeth had earlier found a quantity of old red wool in a drawer in her own home and was knitting a tea-cosy secretly in the mornings before she got up. Tom was clever with his hands and had learned some woodwork at school. He had found a picture of a sheep dog in an old almanac and had found a piece of glass too, just the right size, so he was framing the picture. He worked in the shed where the farm machinery was kept. There was little likelihood of the machinery being used in snowy weather. Elspeth played sentinel for him.

After breakfast on Christmas Day the children shyly presented their gifts.

"Just what we were needing! The old tea-cosy's full of holes," Aunt Jane beamed at Elspeth.

"That's a right bonnie picture, Tom!" Uncle John declared. "It reminds me of the first sheep dog I ever had. Let's get it fixed on the wall right away."

When the picture was hung in the place of honour over the mantelpiece, Aunt Jane fixed her husband with her eye and said with marked emphasis, "Weel, what about it, John?"

"Oh, aye!" Uncle John pretended to have forgotten, and he clapped his hand to his head. "I'll bring it in."

He stepped outside and brought in the bright blue painted sledge. "It's for both of ye, as it seems just the weather for sledging."

"Oh! Oh!" Tom exclaimed, his breath taken away by delight. "Oh, thank you, Uncle John, and Aunt Jane!"

"Yes, thank you very very much!" Elspeth added.

"Let's go try it now!" Tom said.

"Aye. That low hill just behind the house should be a good place," Uncle John suggested.

"But what about the washing up?" Elspeth demurred.

Aunt Jane waved her away. "Awa wi' you, lassie, and enjoy yourself!"

The children rushed up the hill dragging the sledge, with Flash running excitedly in their wake. Aunt Jane watched them from the window as she washed the dishes. Uncle John took up a drying cloth and said, "I'll lend you a hand."

"Mercy me! What ails ye, John?" she exclaimed.

"Och! It's Christmas!" he said lightly.

Aunt Jane looked at him out of the corner of her eye.

"There they go, careering down the hill! Weel, what d'ye know? There's Flash on the sledge with them!" Uncle John stopped his drying operations to watch.

"I might have known it!" Aunt Jane pretended to be wrathful. "You just came to dry the dishes so you could watch them through the window."

"I couldna' stand here looking and doing nothing or you'd have had something to say," Uncle John replied with a chuckle.

Another toboggan run began down the hill.

"Michty me! They've both spilled out of the sledge and Flash too!" Aunt Jane exclaimed. "They're all lying in a heap!"

"It's all right, lass! They're sorting themselves out and laughing. It's all part of the fun."

Aunt Jane's face suddenly clouded. "John, it'll be an awful bleak house without them when Elspeth's gone home and Kate sends for Tom."

"Cheer up, wumman! You knew Elspeth was only kind of loaned for a time and there's no word o' Kate wanting Tom yet." All the same, Uncle John had a secret sinking feeling too.

8

THE MIRACLE AND THE MARAUDER

SOON THE CHRISTMAS holidays were over; the children went back to school; the snow melted on the lower slopes of the hills and in the valley. The year wore on uneventfully through January to March. Tom gave Flash his daily lessons with the sheep and together they ranged the hillsides with Uncle John at the week-ends. Then, one day, Tom came home from school to feverish activity on the farm.

Uncle John and Andra were busy in the paddock dividing the small field into sections with hurdles. Against the hurdles Uncle John was lashing bundles of straw to make a wind break. Andra was constructing a long kind of shed with other hurdles, sloping them in towards each other to make a roof and lashing them all together.

"What's going on here?" Tom asked.

"We're getting ready for the lambing," Uncle John told him. "Like to lend a hand lashing these bundles of straw to the hurdles, Tom?"

"Will you be bringing the flocks down here again?" Tom asked.

"Only the ewes who are going to have lambs soon. Though the ewes can live the winter out of doors even in bitter weather, when the lambs are born, they're tender young things. If we get any more snow they might die if they're not protected from the bitter weather."

"Are you building these straw fences to keep the wind off?"

"That's the idea, Tom. We drive the ewes into this field and Andra is building the lambing shed where the ewes can give birth to their young ones. The first lambs are due in a week or two and we must be ready for them."

That week-end Tom and Flash helped John Meggetson and Jeff with Andra and his sheep dog to bring down from the hills the batch of ewes that would soon give birth to their lambs. They were turned into the long pens in the paddock. That very night there were several flurries of snow. Before he went to bed, Uncle John laid ready his hand torches and storm-lantern. Andra had come from his cottage and taken up his abode in a small room at the farm where there was a bunk bed.

"There'll be a few sleepless nights ahead of both of them," Aunt Jane remarked.

"Why?" Tom asked.

"Dear knows why, but the ewes always seem to give birth in the middle of the night."

"But does Uncle John have to be there with Andra too?"

"It's usually Andra's job to do the night work, but you'd think birth was as catching as measles sometimes. Several ewes'll have their lambs the same night and then Andra needs some help."

"But do the ewes need *people* to help them when the lambs are born?" Tom looked puzzled.

"Aye, sometimes a ewe needs a helping hand. Sometimes the poor creatures are exhausted after it and then your uncle gives them a warm drink o' milk with maybe a drop of brandy in it. Whiles, too, there are lambs that need looking after, that are weak. Then *I* get the job of bringing them into the kitchen by the fire and feeding them out of a baby's bottle."

Each night, the last thing before he went to bed, Uncle John went round the lambing pens to inspect the ewes that were near their time. After that Andra took over. The first night or two only one or two lambs were born and Andra was able to cope alone. Then there came a night when Tom heard a rush of feet to the door and a peremptory knock.

"I'll need some help, Mr. Meggetson. There are *nine* of the ewes will have their lambs in the next couple of hours."

"I'll be with you in a few minutes," John Meggetson replied, and began to get dressed. Tom slipped out of bed too and into his clothes. From his window he watched his uncle cross the farmyard with his lighted lantern. Tom waited, shivering a little, wondering whether he should follow his Uncle John or not.

Half an hour later John Meggetson came hurrying across the yard, a white bundle in his arms. "Jane! Jane!" he called up the stairs. "I'm sorry, lass, but I'm going to need your help wi' the lambs too. Here's the first o' them!"

Aunt Jane went downstairs in her warm woollen dressing gown. "All right, John! I wasna' sleeping. I was kind of expecting the call."

Tom followed her down the stairs uncertain whether he would be sent back to bed.

"Hullo, Tom!" his uncle said in surprise.

"I—I came down to see if I could be any use," Tom stammered.

His uncle hesitated a moment, then said, "Oh, all right, lad! You can come with me. No doubt you'll be able to make yourself useful."

When they reached the lambing pen Andra was on his knees beside a ewe that was panting with the effort of giving birth to her lamb.

"She's in a pretty poor way, mister," Andra told Meggetson.

Uncle John set his lantern down and stooped beside Andra. Tom stood back in the shadows watching. The two lanterns made twin pools of light over the distressed ewe. She groaned as Andra massaged her gently.

"Looks like a big lamb, Andra," Uncle John commented.

"Aye, she's having a lot of difficulty with it. There's a chance the lamb may no' be born alive."

Every now and again the ewe would give a desperate struggle to get to her feet as if she could run away from the trouble which beset her.

"Right, Andra. You hold her down and I'll do what I can to help her." Uncle John rolled up his shirt sleeves. "Tom, can you hold the lantern so that the light shines on the poor beast."

Uncle John went to work on her with gentle compassionate hands, then, after a few minutes, gave an "Ah!" of satisfaction. "That's better! Here comes the lamb's head now."

From between the flanks of the struggling animal appeared a small black face with bright eyes, then a thrust of white shoulders followed by two white forefeet.

"That's grand! That's grand!" Andra breathed.

"Aye, the ewe'll manage the rest herself now if the lamb's not too weak to help her."

Life, even in the smallest and frailest of animals is a marvellous force. Though the lamb was weak, it began to wriggle. Two or three wriggles, then the hind legs appeared. The lamb tried to stand on its weak little legs but they would not support it. The mother gave a long sigh of

achievement and lay still for a minute. She turned her head
and looked at the lamb. In that moment Tom knew all the
awe and the beauty of birth and the fierce upsurge of joy
that comes with it too. To the small boy, born and bred in
the city, it was a miracle of nature. The tears started un-
bidden to his eyes.

Uncle John held the lamb to the ewe's face and she licked
it tiredly as if to claim it for her own.

"She'll do!" Uncle John said. "I'll give her a drop of

warm milk and brandy and let her lie for a bit. That lamb's right feeble, though. Tom, will you carry him over to your aunt?"

Tom stooped into the circle of light and took the frail lamb from his uncle. A tear splashed on to Uncle John's hands. He looked up in surprise, then his face kindled into a warm smile for Tom.

"You'll do, too, lad," he said in a quiet voice. "Give your aunt a hand first, then you can come back here to help us, if you like."

Tom wrapped the lamb in his jacket and cuddled it close to him as he stepped out into the biting northerly wind. To him the lamb had become a precious thing. He stepped into the welcoming warmth of the kitchen.

"Here's another for you, Aunt Jane."

"Mercy on us! It's a whole flock I'll have here soon!" Aunt Jane took a look at Tom's bundle. "Och, the poor wee thing! Elspeth, here's another one for ye. You'll have to give it a bottle."

Only then Tom noticed Elspeth kneeling by the fire, a lamb in her arms that she was feeding from a baby's bottle. The warm firelight threw a glow on her face and arms. She was intent on her task but she looked up and gave Tom a brief smile. "This one's finishing now. He can go to sleep in the basket. Is that another bottle made up with warm milk, Mrs. Meggetson?"

"Aye, lassie, here you are!"

Elspeth took the lamb from Tom. At first it hardly had strength to draw the milk. Mrs. Meggetson dipped the teat of the bottle in a bowl of sugar. The lamb gave it a feeble lick, then all at once began to pull on the bottle.

"Sugar never fails with babies and what goes for babies often goes for lambs too," Aunt Jane chuckled.

Tom watched Elspeth and the lamb. "Will he be all right?" he asked. "He—he almost didn't live at all."

"Aye, Tom, he'll live now. The spark of life is hard to quench even in these wee things," Aunt Jane told him.

Tom waited till the lamb was fed and put in a blanket in the warm basket by the fire. "I'm going back to help Uncle John now," he said. "He could do with me."

There was a new dignity and gravity about Tom. He had assisted at the miracle of birth and his uncle needed him. In a night Tom had risen to the stature of a man.

The lambing went on for many nights after that. Then, one morning, after a quiet night when no lambs were born, Uncle John went out to look at the ewes which had been turned out on the hillside with their lambs to make room for the next batch of ewes in the lambing pens. He came back with a face black as thunder, carrying two dead lambs with their throats torn and bleeding and the wool of their chests dyed red with their blood.

"Oh!" Elspeth cried, jumping to her feet and pressing her hands in horror to her cheeks. Aunt Jane looked equally concerned.

"They've been savaged?"

"Aye, lass. There's been a killer at work," Uncle John said grimly.

"What kind of a killer, Uncle John?" Tom asked.

"Either a dog running wild among the flocks or a fox. More likely a fox, as we're so far from other houses and our dogs were in the house all night. I think there's a strong smell of a fox on the poor wee animals."

Tom felt the black anger surge in him against the killer as he thought of the pitiful frailty of the lamb he had seen born.

"What'll we do, Uncle John?"

"We'll get him, fox or dog."

"Where did you find them, John?" Aunt Jane nodded at the pitiful little corpses.

"In the low field behind the house."

"The killer dared to come in *so* close to the house?"

"Aye. That makes me think it's a fox. The foxes have been short of food in all this snow. Hunger has made them impudent."

"Did you know which ewes the lambs belonged to?"

"There was one standing by the fence near to the dead lambs. She was fair exhausted but there was still a spark of fight in her. She glared at us and lowered her head at Jeff as though she thought *he* was the enemy."

"So ewes really do fight for their lambs," Tom remarked.

"Oh, yes! A ewe would stand up to a lion to save her lambs. Aye, but the foxes are crafty. It's always the ewe wi' *twin* lambs they attack."

"Why is that?" Tom asked.

"Because she canna' defend both lambs at once. She'll stamp and butt at the fox as this one did. The snow was trodden down flat with hoof marks through to the turf below, so the poor beast had put up a good fight for them. The fox would nip in between the lambs and their mother and seize one while the mother was defending the other."

"How will you catch the fox, Uncle John?"

"If the fox can be crafty, so can we! Jane, have you got a tasty bit of meat with a good smell that might attract the killer?"

"Yes, there's a bit rabbit left from the stew."

"Just the thing! There's a weak point in the wire fence, —a hole where I think the fox got in. We'll put the meat near the gap to entice the fox. Come along, Tom! I'll want you and Flash to help me."

"Flash too?" Tom asked eagerly.

"Aye. He's an intelligent wee dog and he's got a quicker turn o' speed than Jeff, He'll know what's wanted."

When they reached the lambing pens with Flash, Uncle John said, "Now this is a bit of a delicate operation. That ewe in the far pen had twin lambs two days ago. I want Flash to help shift her and the lambs into the field where the other lambs were killed last night. Flash'll have to handle her cautiously. She'll be ready to defend her lambs and she might run at him. Can you direct Flash? He'll take his commands better from you."

"I'll do my best," Tom replied.

Uncle John opened the gate of the pen and Tom showed Flash the ewe with her lamb. "Fetch her out, Flash!" Tom said. "Steady now!"

Flash eyed the ewe and went inside the pen.

"Down, Flash!" Tom called.

Flash crouched down, keeping his eye fixed on the sheep.

"Come behind, Flash!"

The little dog moved a few paces to the right of the pen and the sheep moved out of her corner and along the other side of the pen towards the gate.

"That's the way of it!" Uncle John said softly.

"Come round, Flash!" Tom circled his arm.

Flash moved behind the ewe to drive her nearer the gate. Suddenly the ewe turned and stamped at him.

"Down, Flash!" Tom called at once. Flash crouched on his stomach keeping a baleful eye on the ewe which backed away from him. The game of advance and retreat went on, a few paces at a time, Flash moving quietly in response to Tom's commands, never taking his eyes off the sheep.

"He's got the power of the eye all right, that one!" Uncle John said with approval.

At last Flash got the sheep and her lambs through the gate without alarming her unduly. From there it was an easier matter to drive them both into the larger field behind the houses. There were patches of green turf showing through the snow. Soon the ewe was grazing quietly on a patch near the hole in the fence, with her lambs close to her.

"That was a piece of good work, Tom. Flash handled them well."

Tom glowed with pride at his uncle's rare praise.

"Keep the sheep there while I bring a stake and a rope," John Meggetson instructed him.

When Meggetson returned he drove the stake into the ground about twenty-five yards from the hole in the fence, then he secured the ewe to it by a long rope which allowed her to range freely for a few yards round about.

"There, Tom! That's our decoy, the ewe and her lambs. They say the killers come back to the scene of the crime. Tonight we'll keep watch and wait for the killer, fox or dog, to come back to worry another lamb."

"Where shall we keep watch?" Tom asked.

Uncle John pointed to a small building which jutted out from the back of the farm. "The old stable. There's a window there we can open. I'll have my shotgun at the ready there and Flash will do the rest."

"How?" Tom asked.

"You'll see, lad."

That night, as soon as it was dark, John Meggetson put the piece of rabbit down near the hole in the fence. Then he and Tom took up their stations in the old stable with Flash on the lead. Uncle John gave his instructions about Flash and warned Tom, "We might have to wait quite a long time, keeping very still and not talking."

Flash crouched at Tom's feet. The door was slightly

ajar so they could get out quickly with as little noise as possible. Uncle John had his gun resting on the window ledge. From there he could cover all the area round the ewe and her lambs. The moon rose and bathed the field in a pale light, making the shadows a deeper black.

Tom was beginning to feel cold and cramped when Flash suddenly stood up stiff-legged and pointed his nose towards the door. Tom held his muzzle so he would make no sound.

"He's heard something," Uncle John whispered. "Be ready to unleash him when I say the word." He peered through the window, watching the moonlit meadow. "I think there's something stirring in the shadow of the hedge."

They held their breath as they watched the slinking form emerge through the hole, stop and sniff at the rabbit and pull a mouthful or two of the meat from it. Then it seemed as if the sleepy ewe had a premonition of danger. She saw the crouching form of her enemy in the moonlight and tossed her head and gave a snort of alarm. The fox looked up quickly from the rabbit and saw a prey that interested him even more in the twin lambs cowering by their mother's side. He began to move towards them with bared teeth. The ewe went mad with fear and rage. She stamped and snorted, lowering her head to butt the fox if he came nearer. The fox crouched, waiting his moment to dart in and snatch a lamb.

"Now!" Uncle John whispered to Tom. "Send Flash along the hedge between the fox and the hole in the netting."

Tom unleashed Flash and hissed at him. "Away here!" and pointed with his stick towards the hedge. Like a streak of lightning Flash sped along under cover of the hedge. The fox heard him, left the sheep and turned to dash for his escape hole. Flash was there before him, racing up and down in front of it with bared teeth and a menacing growl. The

fox turned and fled in the opposite direction, making for
the gate by the old stable. His flight brought him directly
under Uncle John's line of fire. Uncle John had his finger
ready on the trigger. The shot rang out. The fox leaped
into the air, then rolled over and lay still.

"That's put paid to the killer!" Uncle John said grimly.

Flash was sniffing and growling at his fallen enemy
when Tom slipped the lead on him again. As Uncle John
stooped to pick up the body of the fox, he patted Flash on
the head. "Weel done, Flash! If you hadn't headed the fox
off so neatly, I couldna' have shot him."

Flash flicked out his tongue and licked him, then turned
to Tom and rolled over at his feet. It was as though he knew
that together they had vanquished the enemy of the sheep
that were in his charge.

As soon as the snows were gone the sheep and their lambs
were taken to range the hills again. When Tom was not
at school there was plenty of work for both him and Flash.
Flash showed a wonderful turn of speed in rounding up the
sheep, but what pleased John Meggetson most was Flash's
ready obedience to Tom's commands.

"They make a good pair," Meggetson told Jane. "But
ye've no' to tell Tom that, for I don't want him to get
swelled headed. A swelled headed master makes a swelled
headed dog and that would spoil both of them for the Sheep
Dog Trials."

"D'ye think Flash'll stand a chance?" Jane asked eagerly.

"Maybe! But dogs can get excited and do silly things.
There's no harm in Tom entering him for the local Sheep
Dog Trials at the beginning of July and we'll see how Flash
shapes then."

As the month of May drew to a close in warm summer-like weather, the work of shearing the sheep began. Shearing pens were erected in the paddock and the sheep brought down in batches the previous night to the farm steading. To Tom's surprise his uncle turned the sheep into the old byre and closed the door on them instead of leaving them in the open paddock. Tom asked why this was done.

"A sheep canna' be sheared if its wool is wet," Uncle John explained, "so they're kept under cover the night before shearing."

The next day the actual shearing began. Jeff shepherded a small flock into the pen and the gate was shut on them. Then the inner gate into the shearing space was opened. The sheep bunched together and seemed unwilling to move, but Jeff assumed a threatening attitude behind them and the sheep surged forward. One pushed its way through the gate into the shearing enclosure and Andra shut the gate smartly. The sheep was seized by John Meggetson who heaved it over on to its side and got to work with the clippers.

Tom watched fascinated. The sharp electric clippers stripped the wool off the sheep all in one piece like a jacket. Uncle John got the sheep between his knees and sheared the wool on the chest and legs very carefully, then a pull and a heave and he had the sheep over on its other side. He sheared down towards the tail. Astonished, Tom cried, "Why, the whole fleece has come off in one piece like a coat!"

Andra spread the fleece flat on the ground, put any short locks of wool in the middle, then rolled the fleece up into a bundle and tied it up. Another sheep was let through from the paddock to the shearing pen.

Tom gazed after the shorn sheep. "How thin it looks!"

"Aye, I reckon its own mother would hardly know it!"

Uncle John grinned. "Like to give Andra a hand bringing the sheep through from the paddock?"

All this time Flash sat behind Tom. He watched Jeff controlling the sheep and now and again he gave an eager little whine.

"All right, Flash! You shall have your turn soon," Uncle John promised him.

When Flash's turn came he ushered the batch of sheep in a quiet, methodical fashion into the pen and under Tom's directions he got them moving towards the gate into the shearing pen. They hesitated and bunched together as if dreading the ordeal of having their coats removed and their thin ribs exposed. They headed in all directions but the right one. Flash ran round them and skilfully detached one sheep that seemed to be causing the most trouble. He "wore" the sheep this way and that till he got him through the open gate to Mr. Meggetson.

"Well done, Flash! You shed that sheep like a veteran! That dog uses his brains," he told Tom. "As soon as we've done shearing we'll start on giving Flash a thorough training for the Trials."

Thereafter every evening and most of Saturday was spent in giving Flash his intensive training. Uncle John outlined to Tom what Flash would have to do at the Trials.

"There's nothing the dog hasn't done already in practice. He'll have five sheep to work with."

"Only five!" Tom exclaimed. "Why, Flash can bring in a whole flock!"

"Maybe, but it's five sheep each dog has to run on in the Trials. He'll have to make an outrun of four hundred yards, either to right or left, so practise both."

Tom nodded. "Then Flash has to lift the sheep down towards me?"

"That's right, but he has to send them through centre gates seven yards wide, about one hundred and fifty yards from where you will be standing."

"Flash has brought sheep through narrower spaces than that."

"Aye, but *style* counts for a lot, Tom. He mustn't let a sheep get away from him round the posts. Then, the next thing, he has to bring the sheep in a cross drive right across the course through two sets of gates at opposite sides, then back to where you are standing. There'll be two posts set up where you are to stand."

Tom nodded. "What next?"

"You'll be at the forward post by then and he must bring the sheep round behind you."

"Yes, and then?"

"There's a circle twenty-five feet across near your post which is called the shedding ring. Flash will have to drive his five sheep into that. There he has to separate two of the sheep from the five and do it inside the circle."

"I think he could do that all right."

"Yes, so do I. Then comes penning the sheep."

"He's had plenty of practice in that," Tom said with satisfaction. "What's the size of the pen?"

"Nine feet by six feet, and one side of it is a gate. You'll have a six-foot rope by which to hold the gate open. You've got to stay at the end of the rope. Ye can speak to the dog, but no' help him in any way to drive the sheep in. When he's got the sheep in, ye can swing the gate shut."

"Is that the end of the competition?" Tom asked.

"Oh no! Flash will have to bring the sheep out o' the pen back to you in the ring and separate one sheep from the rest. Ye'll be able to point it out to him and that sheep'll be marked by a red ribbon."

"Flash has singled out one sheep before now and without a ribbon."

"True!" Uncle John agreed. "But, the whole job from the outrun has to be done inside fifteen minutes."

Tom let out a low whistle. "Flash has lots of speed, though."

"Aye, but it doesn't depend on speed alone, mark you! The dog that gets most marks from the judges will be the one which moves the sheep quietly and steadily. He mustn't rush the sheep or scatter them. Ye won't have to give him too many commands, either." Uncle John finished on a word of caution. "*Fuss* is what spoils many a performance."

Uncle John and Tom marked out the lower field as though it were the competition ground and even built a pen on it. After that Tom spent every spare moment of his time in training Flash. He taught the dog to obey his whistle as well as his word of command. Elspeth usually watched the training too, standing on the gate into the field to see Flash's performance better. If, but only if, Flash had done well, she was allowed to give him *one* chocolate drop, but only after she had asked Tom's permission. Flash knew this was his reward for working well and he would look from Tom to Elspeth and back, waiting to see if he would be rewarded.

"You know, Elspeth, Flash tries harder if you're watching him," Tom declared.

"I think the three of them make a kind of team, Tom, Flash and Elspeth," Uncle John confided in Aunt Jane. "There's no word o' the lassie going back hame yet, is there?"

Aunt Jane shook her head. "When Mr. Young was up here at the week-end he said Alison might have to stay at the Convalescent Home a wee while yet. She's to have massage and all kinds of electrical treatment."

"Though I hope Alison gets better quickly, I'm no' wanting to lose the lassie either. I hope she's able to stay till after the Sheep Dog Trials anyway. There's no denying both Tom and Flash do better when Elspeth's looking on."

Aunt Jane nodded her head sagely. "You see, Elspeth *believes* in Tom and Flash, and Tom knows it and it gives him confidence. He thinks a lot of Elspeth's good opinion."

"Aye, and when Tom has confidence, so has Flash! It's as though Flash can read Tom's thoughts at times." He sat silent for a moment or two, then said, "There's been no word from America for a while. I wonder if Kate ever *will* send for the lad?"

Aunt Jane folded up her knitting. "With Elspeth gone home and Tom in America, we're going to be a right lonely old couple again, John Meggetson. I don't think we're going to like it."

THE SHEEP DOG TRIALS

ONE MORNING, JUST before the Sheep Dog Trials, the telephone rang with sharp insistence. Mr. Meggetson took the call. "It's for you, Elspeth," he said, handing her the receiver.

Elspeth listened, then said quietly, "All right, father! I'll come home at once and get the house ready." She put down the receiver and told them, "Mother is coming home tomorrow, but she'll only be able to be up part of the day at first. I'll have to go home right away, Mrs. Meggetson."

"Aye, lassie, your duty's to your mother," Aunt Jane agreed, "We're all going to miss you, though."

Without Elspeth the house seemed quiet and dull. Tom missed her most of all during the training sessions with Flash. She had always been there, leaning on the gate to watch and to give Flash that word of praise that he loved. Flash missed her too and went hunting around the farm as if trying to find her.

The time came for Tom to take Flash through his final rehearsals before the Trials.

"Oh, bother! He's singled the wrong sheep out," Tom cried in vexation. "He's never done that before! If he does that on Saturday he'll lose all our chances of winning. You silly dog, Flash!" There was a note of anger in Tom's voice. Flash looked up at him unhappily. He came to Tom with his head hanging down, dismayed.

"You're both tired and the practice has gone on too long," Uncle Jim remarked. "I think Flash is missing Elspeth and her chocolate drops as well."

"Maybe we're *both* missing Elspeth. Things went right when she was there! Why did she have to go away just before the Trials?" Tom burst out.

Uncle John threw Tom a searching glance, but said nothing more. That night, when Tom had gone to bed, he put through a telephone call.

The Saturday of the Sheep Dog Trials broke bright with sunshine and a light breeze. Breakfast was early, for the Trials were to be held at a park some miles away, and the qualifying runs were to begin at 8.30 a.m. Uncle John brought out the Land Rover.

Aunt Jane came out of the house resplendent in a floral silk dress with a navy-blue corded silk coat that smelled faintly of camphor. To crown it and herself, she wore a navy straw hat bedecked with rosebuds. Uncle John stared at her as if beholding a vision.

"Guid sakes, Jane! Where did you get that rig from? I've never seen you in that before."

Aunt Jane looked at him pityingly. "It's a shame you're getting so old that your memory's failing! I wore this at our Meg's wedding five years ago."

"Michty me! So you did!" Uncle John exclaimed.

"Even if you like going round like a tramp there's no call for me to look an old frump," Aunt Jane told him. "One of us has got to show folk the family isn't in the Poor's House."

Uncle John drove the car to the parking field for the Trials, then they made their way to the ground. The spectators were standing on a small hill that overlooked the course. Some of them had brought car rugs on which their families sat. Aunt Jane spread her rug in an advantageous position near to the rope that divided the spectators from the course. Everywhere farmers and shepherds were standing in little groups with their dogs at their feet. Just in front of the rope was the judges' tent.

Tom and Aunt Jane settled down on the ground Flash lay down at Tom's feet. He kept looking about him as though searching for someone all the time. The warm smell of the meadow was wafted towards them mingled with the sharper scent of dogs and sheep. Uncle John went to get a printed programme to see what place Tom had drawn.

"You've drawn fifth place in your heat," he told Tom.

"I'm glad I've not drawn first," Tom said with relief. "I wouldn't have known what to do."

"You watch the competitors before you and you'll see how it goes," his uncle advised him. "Let Flash watch too!"

Flash sat bolt upright, never taking his eyes off the competing dogs. It was as though he was learning what to do at the Trials too. Once, when a sheep eluded the dog to escape round the hurdles, Flash gave what seemed like a critical sniff. At last their turn came.

When Tom took the field with Flash there were interested comments from the spectators.

"That's a very young laddie to be competing."

"Aye, and the dog's quite a young one too."

"Whose lad is he?"

"Nephew to Birkhope. He's been living with them close on a year. The dog belongs to him, so I've heard."

"Weel, I don't suppose he'll do much but we all have to learn the know-how. This'll be an experience for the boy."

Uncle John, who overheard this speech, turned and

winked at Aunt Jane. "Only let Tom and Flash get through the qualifying round and we'll see what they can do."

"Do you think he'll win into the Final, John? It means so much to Tom, more for Flash's sake than his own." Aunt Jane sounded anxious.

"You never can tell. Either of them might do something silly. So far, though, there's no' been over-much talent in the other dogs."

Tom felt a lonely figure as he stood beside the post, stick in hand and with Flash at his feet, waiting for the signal from the judge. It seemed as if the eyes of the spectators were boring into his back. He stooped and patted Flash to give them both more confidence. Flash responded with his quick grateful lick to the hand.

"Do your best for us, Flash! Tom said in a low voice. "Now look at the sheep, lad." He pointed to the distant sheep that Flash was to bring in, and Flash crouched in readiness.

The judge's whistle blew. Back in his spectator's seat Uncle John started his stop-watch.

"Away here, Flash!" Tom's voice rang out clearly and his stick pointed the direction. Flash never hesitated but was away like the wind and in behind the flock.

"A lovely outrun, that!" Uncle John said with satisfaction.

Tom gave the whistle which mean "Down!" and at once Flash crouched behind the little flock.

There was a murmur of surprised admiration from the spectators.

Flash approached the sheep and began to "lift" them towards Tom. The sheep were not so docile as the Birkhope flocks and were inclined to scatter. Flash went after them and brought them together again. Owing to the friskiness of the flock Tom had to take more time over the drive than usual. He gave the whistle "Down!" more frequently than he did at home and had Flash crouching behind his five sheep more times than usual.

Uncle John looked anxiously at his stop-watch. "He's taking his time," he breathed uneasily to Aunt Jane. "I hope he's remembered there's a time limit."

The sheep had steadied, however, under Flash's powerful compelling eye and he brought all five quite neatly through the first gate and round behind Tom. Next came the cross drive, and again Tom seemed to be taking a long time over it, making sure that the sheep did not scatter. Still Uncle John consulted his watch uneasily.

Flash gathered the sheep in the shedding ring and divided them into two groups as the test required. This took some time. One of the sheep almost got away out of the ring, though, and Flash's bunching of the group afterwards was not so neat as he had done it many times before on the farm. Likewise he got through the penning test with little difficulty, though again Flash seemed to take his time. Tom let the gate swing shut with a thankful heart.

Uncle John again looked anxiously at his watch. "There's only the singling of the sheep now. If Flash gets to business quickly, he might just make it," he whispered to Aunt Jane.

Tom himself realized that Flash had taken longer than usual over some of the tasks and he re-opened the pen gate hurriedly, then went and took up his stance at the shedding ring. Flash bundled the sheep out of the pen to the shedding ring, though they were rather restive there and time was wasted in keeping them together. When Tom pointed to the be-ribboned sheep, however, Flash had little difficulty in singling him out and holding him at the far side of the shedding ring.

The judge's whistle sounded to show that the test was

over. Uncle John looked for the last time at his stop watch. "He's just made it," he said, breathing a sigh of relief.

Tom stooped and patted Flash and from the crowd of spectators there came clapping and a shout of "Weel done, lad!"

Tom heaved a sigh of relief that the first trial was over.

"How did we do?" Tom whispered to his uncle.

"No' bad!" Uncle John told him. "You nearly ran out o' time though, Tom. Ye were slow at getting off your mark at the 'lift' and in bringing them down the field."

"I know," Tom said ruefully. "The sheep were rather lively, though, and I daren't risk Flash scattering them"

"Fair enough!" Uncle John agreed, "But Flash was no' showing the spark he usually does. If ye get through to the final, ye'll need to make better time there."

"Shall we get through to the final?" Tom asked rather despondently.

"That I can't tell ye, Tom, till the marks for all the dogs are known, and that'll no' be for another hour yet. Take heart, lad! From what I saw, ye've at least got a chance."

Tom and Flash watched the rest of the Qualifying Trials in a kind of dream, Tom alternately fluctuating between hope and despair that Flash would get a place in the Final. At last the heats were over and the judges went to their tent to compare their findings. It seemed an eternity to Tom before they emerged. The chief judge made his announcements through a megaphone. Six dogs had been chosen to compete in the finals in the afternoon. Everyone waited with bated breath to know which dogs had been successful. Tom went quite pale. The judge shuffled his papers and seemed to have mislaid the very one he wanted. At last he found it, cleared his voice, and began to read out the names. Tom clenched his fists so tightly that his nails dug into the palms of his hands. Four names were read out, but Flash's was not among them. Then came the fifth. "Flash, owned by Tom Stokes."

Tom could hardly believe his ears. He let out a tremendous breath of relief. Uncle John slapped him hard on the back.

"You've made it, Tom! You've made the final!" Uncle John was no less pleased than Tom.

"Oh, Flash! Flash!" Tom hugged the dog to him.

The dog knew that Tom was pleased with him and licked his face with the warm affection that only a dog can show.

At the same time he looked round about Tom as if missing something.

"He's looking for Elspeth," Tom said. "Elspeth always praised him when he did well."

"Weel, now, ye'll be wanting some food," Uncle John said briskly. "You and Tom go to the marquee, Jane, and get some dinner. See that you get a drink of water for Flash, Tom, but don't give him anything to eat, not till he's run in the Final."

"Aren't you coming for dinner with us too, Uncle John?" Tom asked, slightly disappointed.

"No—er—I've got to go and see someone. See you later on just here before the Finals begin," he said in a vague kind of voice and strode away in the direction of the car park.

"Come on, Tom! We may have to queue for places at the tables," Aunt Jane said.

With a reluctant backward glance at his uncle, Tom whistled Flash to heel and they set out for the refreshment tent.

After lunch people began to take up their positions overlooking the course again. Tom and Aunt Jane were just taking their seats on the rug when Uncle John reappeared. A smaller figure followed in his wake. *It was Elspeth!* Tom jumped to his feet with delight. "Elspeth! It's you! I didn't know you were coming!"

"Your uncle came to fetch me." Elspeth bubbled over with joy too. "He rang up Father last night, and Mother said she could spare me this afternoon."

"Has Uncle John told you Flash is in the Final?"

"Yes, he did! Oh, Tom, I'm so glad!"

Flash leaped for joy about her feet, licking at her hands. She bent to pat and hug him. "Oh, Flash, you're a wonder dog!"

Suddenly Flash sniffed at her pocket.

"You crafty one, Flash! You know I've got your choco-late drops in this pocket," Elspeth laughed. "Do well in the Final, and you'll have your reward."

Flash gave an excited bark as if showing he understood.

"We shall both do better now you're here, Elspeth," Tom said.

Tom had drawn the fourth place to run in the Final. Elspeth went with them as far as the post where Tom was to stand, gave Flash a pat and said, "Do your best, Flash, there's a good dog!" and withdrew again behind the rope.

Tom took up his position at the first post with far more confidence than he had felt in the morning. He pointed the far-away sheep out to Flash and they waited for the judge's whistle. Almost before the words "Away there!" came from Tom, Flash was off like a streak of lightning.

"See that!" came voices from the crowd, amazed at the speed of the dog.

In a second or two Flash was behind the flock and at Tom's whistle he dropped down, crawling towards them on his stomach so as not to alarm them. Tom hardly needed to give him any commands. He came stealthily towards the little flock of five sheep. As soon as they were aware of him they began to move down the hill. To Tom's relief they went quietly, not in the least fussed, but obedient.

"Oh, grand! Grand!" Uncle John breathed, not even bothering to look at his stop-watch. "He'll get good marks for that."

Flash turned the sheep neatly between the posts and down to Tom, who then advanced to the second post.

Then came the cross-drive which he executed with skill, manœuvring even the stupid outside sheep through the two gates without any bother. He brought them in a tidy bunch to the shedding ring. This time, when Tom pointed out the sheep to be shed, there was little hesitation. Flash went in close and crouched before the small flock which parted, three to one side and two to the other. He then turned to the two sheep and brought them out of the ring at Tom's command. One of the sheep turned and stamped at him, but Flash was not to be intimidated. He crouched before it and wore it down with a glaring look.

"Come by!" Tom pointed to the left and motioned to Flash to reunite the five sheep within the ring. Without any further direction from Tom he brought them together again and stood panting a little, his pink tongue flicking in and out, looking for Tom to lead the way to the pen. As soon as Tom held the gate by the rope he was at the heels of the sheep. It was with an air of surprise that they found themselves propelled into the pen. Tom let the gate swing to and gave the sheep just time to breathe and settle before he opened it again. Flash stood with one paw lifted, his eyes on Tom.

"Bring them out, Flash!" was all Tom needed to say quietly and the little dog was at the pen, moving behind the sheep. One sheep, the one who had given trouble before, faced about as if to defy him, but Flash advanced in menacing fashion, glaring at the sheep. It backed away and out to join the other four. Quietly, determinedly, Flash brought them along, running back and forth behind them, darting to the sides to prevent a break-away by the frisky one. When he had them all in the ring before Tom, he had to single out the sheep with the ribbon.

Perhaps it was fortunate that the be-ribboned sheep was the one which had given trouble in the pen. He had been thoroughly subdued already by the masterful look in Flash's eye. When Flash went in close and bent that baleful glare upon him again, he backed away. Flash "wore" him by alternately crouching and moving, never taking his eyes off him. The mesmerized sheep retreated before him till he was separated from the others and arrived at Tom's feet. Even there Flash held him by crouching before him.

The judge's whistle blew and the test was over!

"Grand! Well within his fifteen minutes too!" Uncle John cried with delight. "That dog's a wonder!"

"So is Tom!" Aunt Jane declared, but her remark was lost in the loud applause from the spectators.

Tom stooped and gave Flash the well earned pat and said "Good dog, Flash! Good dog!" Flash gave his hand the usual quick lick, then he looked beyond Tom with searching eyes. There was Elspeth waiting on the rope fence, just as she had watched and waited so often at the farm. Flash gave a little yelp of delight though he still kept obediently to heel behind Tom. When they left the field Elspeth went down on her knees and hugged the dog.

"Oh, well done, Flash! And well done, you too, Tom! It was just marvellous."

"I think Flash did so well because he knew you were watching him." Tom told her. "He always does better when you are there."

Uncle John came up and shook Tom by the hand. "Man, Tom, I'm proud of you," he said.

Flash was looking up expectantly at Elspeth.

"Mercy me! I almost forgot!" she exclaimed. "Mr. Meggetson, do you think I could give Flash a chocolate drop?"

"*One* chocolate drop! You can give him *three*." John Meggetson said recklessly.

When the last of the trials was over, after a brief interval, the judges announced their decision.

"Two dogs came very close in the final award of marks," the spokesman told the spectators gathered round the judges' tent, "These were Mr. Morrison's 'Laddie' and Mr. Tom Stokes' 'Flash'."

Tom's heart missed a beat with excitement and Elspeth's cheeks went pink.

"On the aggregate of marks, however, leading by two marks only, the prize is awarded to Flash, owned by Mr. Tom Stokes. We would specially like to commend Flash for his speedy outrun and the controlled way he gathered and lifted the sheep, and Mr. Tom Stokes for the quiet way he gave his commands. May I say that for a lad he did remarkably well. We think that if both boy and dog go on in the same way, someday Peebleshire may produce a new national champion."

There was loud applause at this last remark. Tom could hardly believe that the judge was speaking about him.

"I have to add that the Cup for the youngest competitor goes to Tom Stokes and Flash also. And now I will ask Mistress Ogilvie if she will kindly present the prizes. Will each prize-winner kindly come up as his name is announced, and bring his dog with him?"

"Go on, lad!" Uncle John said, giving Tom a little push when his name was called.

Feeling that he was in a dream, Tom advanced to the tent with Flash at his heels. He shook hands with Mistress Ogilvie, putting a rather grubby and sticky hand into hers. Mistress Ogilvie gave him a very friendly smile as she presented him with his two silver cups and a cheque for three guineas which she tucked into one silver cup for him. Tom turned back to his uncle and aunt. The silver cups were much admired and Aunt Jane took charge of the cheque in her handbag at Tom's request. Uncle John kept introducing

Tom with pride to his farmer friends. At last they broke away and made for the car park. As they went Uncle John was waylaid by a stranger. The others waited by the car while Uncle John talked to him, then, to their surprise, Uncle John brought the man along to the car.

"This is Mr. McKay, the dog dealer," he said in a reserved voice. "This is my nephew, Tom Stokes, who owns Flash."

"Your dog put up an excellent performance in the Final," Mr. McKay told Tom. "Do you think of selling him at all?"

"Oh, no!" Tom said at once, putting his arms around Flash.

"Well, lad, hear what I'm offering before you turn it down point-blank. I'll give you a hundred pounds for the dog."

Tom caught his breath in amazement. A hundred pounds! It sounded untold riches.

"It's a deal of money, Tom," his uncle told him soberly. "It would give you a good start in America if ever you went to Kate."

Tom's face clouded. He hugged Flash to him, saying nothing. Aunt Jane looked at him and put in her word. "Mr. McKay, you can't expect Tom to make up his mind at a snap of the fingers. You must give him time to think it over."

"Aye, that's right," Uncle John agreed. "This needs talking about first. Let us have your telephone number and when Tom has made up his mind, he can phone you."

"Fair enough!" Mr. McKay wrote his telephone number on an envelope and gave it to Tom. "You can phone me any time this evening, laddie."

Tom was so quiet on the journey home that Elspeth cast several questioning glances at him, as they sat in the rear seat of the car with Flash at their feet.

"What's wrong, Tom?" she asked at last in a whisper.

"I'm wondering whether I ought to sell Flash," he said in a low voice of utter misery.

"Sell Flash? Do you mean you'd rather have a hundred pounds than Flash?" Elspeth sounded amazed.

"Of course I wouldn't! But a hundred pounds would pay my fare to America."

"Why? Has your sister sent for you?" A chill feeling swept over Elspeth.

"Not yet! Maybe Uncle John *wants* me to sell Flash. He said the hundred pounds would give me a good start in America. Perhaps he's tired of having me at Birkhope.". .

"Tom Stokes, how can you think that?" Elspeth hissed at him. The whole conversation was conducted in whispers for fear Uncle John and Aunt Jane might overhear in the front seat. "Haven't they made you welcome at Birkhope? Don't be stupid! Besides, *you* don't want to sell Flash, do you? And he belongs to *you*."

"If I sell Flash, no one and nothing will ever belong to me again." The words broke from Tom's heart.

Elspeth refrained from saying anything. There was no use talking to Tom in that mood, but she had made up her mind what she must do.

Aunt Jane spoke over her shoulder. "You've to come to supper with us, Elspeth. Mr. Meggetson will drive you home afterwards."

When they got out of the car Uncle John said, "While you're getting the supper ready I'll just take a look at the cows and see if Andra's got by all right with the milking."

Elspeth followed Aunt Jane and lent a hand first in setting the table. She watched her opportunity and slipped out to the byre.

"Mr. Meggetson, could I have a word with you?" she asked.

"Yes, lass. What is it?"

"It's about Tom. Do *you* want him to go to America?"

John Meggetson stared at her. "Guid sakes, no! Whatever makes you think that?"

"Tom thinks you do. He's got the idea you're tired of having him at Birkhope," Elspeth told him with her blunt honesty.

"Now what bee has that silly young fool got under his bonnet?" Uncle John exclaimed irately.

"He thinks you want him to sell Flash to pay his fare to America."

"Surely not?" Uncle John swung round, startled.

"You did tell him it would give him a good start there. But you do want him to stay here, really, don't you, Mr. Meggetson?" Elspeth said quietly.

"Of course I do! I don't mind telling you, Elspeth, that I don't want to part with him, even to his sister Kate."

"Have you ever told Tom that?"

"Why, no! It—it never occurred to me——"

"Mr. Meggetson, have you never guessed that Tom's grown fond of you, too?"

Uncle John opened his eyes wide. "Do you think so, lass? Why, Tom's become a kind of son to me and his aunt."

"Then will you please go in and tell him that at once, Mr. Meggetson, before he speaks to Mr. McKay on the phone and sells Flash and breaks his heart over it."

Mr. Meggetson looked shocked. "Sell Flash? I'll go and sort the young idiot at once!" He turned and strode into the house with Elspeth at his heels.

He went straight to Tom in the kitchen. "Look here, Tom! You and I have got to have a talk and come to an understanding."

Tom thought with a sinking heart, "Now he's going to tell me I must sell Flash and go to America."

"Did *you* think I wanted you to leave Birkhope and go to America? I want the truth now. There must be the truth between us over this."

"Well,—yes," Tom faltered.

"And you thought I wanted you to sell Flash to pay your fare?"

Tom swallowed. "I thought perhaps that's what I should do if you wanted me to go."

"Then you're just a young fool!" Uncle John barked. "Can you no' understand that I've grown used to having you around?—That I *like* having you here, and that I'm not wanting you to go to America?"

Tom's eyes widened. "Oh, Uncle John! Do you mean that?"

"Of course I do!" Uncle John glared at him fiercely.

At the raised voices Flash suddenly came between them and looked from one to another and uttered a low growl. He looked so perplexed that they both burst out laughing and the strain was broken.

"Well, that's settled, thanks to Elspeth!" Aunt Jane said briskly. "Now draw up your chairs to the table and we'll have our supper."

She put on her apron to protect her best dress and an envelope fell out of the pocket.

"Mercy me! Here's a letter that come just before we left the house! I stuck it in my pocket without looking at it. It'll be from Meg." She took another look at the address. "Why, no! It's for Tom."

Tom turned the letter over. It bore an American stamp. "It's from Kate."

"You read it while I'm pouring the tea," Aunt Jane said.

When she passed Tom his cup, he was staring at the letter as as though mesmerised.

"Weel, what's the news from Kate?" Aunt Jane said sharply.

"She—she says they're moving into a larger apartment and there might be room for me there. She says she *thinks* she can persuade Hymer to have me, but it'll take a time to save the fare."

Uncle John looked troubled. "How do you feel about going to America now, Tom?"

"Could I take Flash to America?" Tom asked.

"You could, but he might have to stay in quarantine before you could have him with you."

"Flash would be miserable in quarantine, and I don't think Kate would want him in her apartment," Tom declared. "I'm not going! I don't want to part with Flash and—and I don't want to leave you and Aunt Jane either."

Uncle John and Aunt Jane looked at each other and smiled.

"I—I don't think Kate will miss me, really. She's got Hymer. I might be in the way. Besides, I feel I *belong* here."

"That's how we feel, too, Tom," Aunt Jane said gently. "Now, let's be getting on with our suppers. Bless the lad! What's taken him now?" she cried as Tom jumped up from his chair.

"Please, I want to telephone Mr. McKay, Uncle John," Tom said, taking the envelope from his pocket. "I'm going to tell him that Flash is *not* for sale and that not even a *thousand* pounds would buy him!"

TURK THE BORDER COLLIE

After the death of his master, Turk is sent to a faraway farm to finish his sheep-dog training. But the longing for 'Old David' and familiar fields is so powerful that he runs away and tries to find his way home again. His adventures and companions on the way are many and varied until at last, barely alive, he returns to where he was born.

Kathleen Fidler based Turk on a sheep dog from the Borders who was chosen to play the part of Flash in the film of *Flash the Sheep Dog*, also available as a *Kelpie* paperback.

'*Turk the Border Collie* is a worthy successor to *Flash*, for no one quite equals Kathleen Fidler in the creation of dog personalities.' *The Scotsman*